Weston smiled broadly as Hayden lifted him from his crib and carried him to the diaper table.

He kicked and squirmed and made delighted baby sounds while Hayden changed his diaper.

"Want to walk?" Hayden scooped the boy up then put his feet on the ground.

For the first time, Weston noticed Lizzie in the doorway. He waved at her, his little fingers opening and closing.

Then he turned into Hayden's chest, peeking at her once, then again and giggling.

"Are you playing peekaboo with me?" Lizzie asked, kneeling on the floor and covering her face with her hands, then peeking around them.

He giggled again. "Boo!"

She tapped the tip of his nose. "I'm not sure your daddy has told you, but you have the sweetest smile."

As if on cue, Weston smiled at his father. "Da da." Weston squealed, bouncing his little legs and clapping his hands.

Lizzie wasn't sure which was sweeter: Weston's smile or Hayden's devotion to his son.

Or that the entire time they'd been in Weston's nursery, she'd totally forgotten about the storm.

Dear Reader,

I am so excited about this book! Why? It's my very first Special Edition novel, and I'm beyond thrilled to be part of the family! As I'm a Texas girl, my stories have small towns, cowboys and real-life conflict everyone can connect with. I very definitely connected with this story—and these characters.

Welcome to the small town of Granite Falls, Texas. In these parts, ranching is a way of life, neighbors still look out for one another, and the cowboys and their canine companions are true-blue. I'm pretty sweet on the Mitchell brothers, and after you meet Hayden, I hope you will be, too. There's nothing like a man who lets a woman stand on her own two feet—ready and willing to support her, no matter what. That's Hayden, to a T. Lizzie and Hayden might be night and day, but everyone knows you can't have one without the other.

I hope you'll come back to visit Granite Falls again!

Until then, happy reading!

Sasha Summers

The Rancher's Forever Family

SASHA SUMMERS

HARLEQUIN

SPECIAL
EDITION

Recycling programs for this product may not exist in your area.

ISBN-13: 978-1-335-40487-9

The Rancher's Forever Family

Copyright © 2021 by Sasha Best

All rights reserved. No part of this book may be used or reproduced in any manner whatsoever without written permission except in the case of brief quotations embodied in critical articles and reviews.

This is a work of fiction. Names, characters, places and incidents are either the product of the author's imagination or are used fictitiously. Any resemblance to actual persons, living or dead, businesses, companies, events or locales is entirely coincidental.

This edition published by arrangement with Harlequin Books S.A.

For questions and comments about the quality of this book, please contact us at CustomerService@Harlequin.com.

Harlequin Enterprises ULC
22 Adelaide St. West, 40th Floor
Toronto, Ontario M5H 4E3, Canada
www.Harlequin.com

Printed in U.S.A.

Sasha Summers grew up surrounded by books. Her passions have always been storytelling, romance and travel—passions she's used to write more than twenty romance novels and novellas. Now a bestselling and award-winning author, Sasha continues to fall a little in love with each hero she writes. From easy-on-the-eyes cowboys, sexy alpha-male werewolves, to heroes of truly mythic proportions, she believes that everyone should have their happily-ever-after—in fiction and real life.

Sasha lives in the suburbs of the Texas Hill Country with her amazing family. She looks forward to hearing from fans and hopes you'll visit her online: on Facebook at sashasummersauthor, on Twitter, @sashawrites, or email her at sashasummersauthor@gmail.com.

Books by Sasha Summers

Harlequin Western Romance

The Boones of Texas

A Cowboy's Christmas Reunion
Twins for the Rebel Cowboy
Courted by the Cowboy
A Cowboy to Call Daddy
A Son for the Cowboy
Cowboy Lullaby

Harlequin Blaze

Seducing the Best Man
Christmas in His Bed

Visit the Author Profile page
at Harlequin.com for more titles.

Dedicated to all the animal lovers out there.
We know there is no truer love
than that of our animal companions.

And to my beloved Gerard, the Feline Overlord,
I miss you so.

Chapter One

"Think she's going to come inside?" Hayden asked, glancing back at the small red car—and the woman inside—that had been sitting in front of the K-9 Center for the better part of an hour.

His dog, Charley, a Belgian Malinois, answered with a part grumble, part whine and rested his chin on Hayden's knee. As always, Hayden caved to the silent request in the dog's tawny eyes and gave an obliging scratch behind the ear. Charley leaned in, his long tail thumping against the stained concrete floor in an unmistakable thank-you.

"Yeah, I know, you've got it rough." Hayden chuckled, glancing at the clock on the wall. His appointment was already twenty-three minutes behind. Technically she was here—if sitting in her car counted. "We'll be back on the ranch before noon." He had to be there or he'd hear about it later. His mother didn't mind helping out with his eleven-month-old son, Weston, but with any luck, they would be there before his son woke up from his morning nap, needing a change and a bottle. *If* Dr. Elizabeth Vega ever managed to exit her vehicle and actually come inside. His attention returned to the car, beyond curious at this point.

She was slumped forward, forehead resting on the steering wheel, AC blowing hard enough to keep her long dark hair dancing around her. If she hadn't been talking minutes ago—hands flying and head shaking—he might have been worried. At one point, she'd even opened the door. He and Charley had both stood, ready to greet her. Then the car door had slammed shut, Elizabeth Vega still inside.

Because she was *struggling*. That was the word Dr. Mark Sai had used. Several times. Sai was very good at being diplomatic; it was his job. Hayden could remember how careful Sai had been the first few times they'd met. Sai had been the unit psychiatrist who had to determine his overall mental health after every difficult incursion. Hayden had landed on his couch a few times. He hadn't liked it, but Mark tried to make it suck less. So, when Sai called, asking for a favor, Hayden said yes. He was looking for a therapy dog—something to help a patient process a recent trauma and support her return to daily life. Most of the dogs that came through the center were ready for retirement, needed extra care or had medical disabilities. But Sierra was a rare exception.

Hell, Sierra was a rare dog. Steady and reliable, she had a calming effect on her handlers and the people she had worked to save.

It was possible she was just what Dr. Elizabeth Vega needed. Sai hoped so. And while Hayden refused to give his comrade-in-arms a guarantee, he was willing to chance it. If, and only if, what Dr. Vega needed wasn't too much for Sierra to shoulder. Ultimately, Hayden wasn't in the business of healing people—that was Sai's job. His job? Honoring and respecting the service these dogs had given their country.

Only way to know? Get this interview started.

"How about we go check on her?" He pushed himself up from the chair.

Charley jumped up, eyes on him, ears alert.

"Don't get too excited, we're just going outside." With a final glance at the paperwork on his desk, he put his hat on, smoothed a hand over his shirt and headed for the door with Charley at his heels.

The heat greeted them like a punch to the chest, humid-heavy and sweat-inducing. Not that he minded. After two tours with forty-five pounds or more strapped onto his back, little things like triple-digit heat didn't bother him. Or Charley. Considering what they'd been through together, not much got to them.

But when Elizabeth Vega looked up and he saw the raw panic on her face… Well, it got to him. A hell of a lot. So much so that he stopped walking right there, in the middle of the damn parking lot.

Maybe it was her posture, bowed up and defensive. Maybe it was how big her eyes got when she saw him standing there. Or how her grip, knuckles white already, tightened on the steering wheel. He knew fear when he saw it. Question was, what was she afraid of and what was he supposed to do about it?

She said something, shook her head and took a deep breath. The car turned off. The door opened. But she didn't get out.

"Well, hell," he mumbled, doing his best to look normal. Meaning not in the least bit intimidating. His brothers and his squad agreed that was impossible—and liked reminding him of it every chance they got. He was big, stern and careful with his words. All of which served him well when he'd been in the service. Being nice and smiley and in touch with your feelings? Not his thing. At all. He was working on that. In order to do this job, to interact with people and screen adoption applicants, he needed to be approachable. Normal. Pleasant even. And he was trying. For the dogs—it was always about the dogs. They'd served honorably and had the right to a loving forever home. And today Sierra, one of the sweetest white Labs he'd ever trained, might be meeting "her person"—if this woman was worthy of her.

From what he'd seen so far, that point was up for negotiation.

With five long strides, he was by the car door, stooping to peer inside. "Need a hand?"

She shook her head, dark curls bouncing. "No."

The rhythmic whir of cicadas grew deafening the longer he stood there, waiting. And waiting. And sweating.

Since it was rude to stare, he tried not to. But that didn't stop him from noticing details. He was trained for that. Cues. Subtleties. The bright peach nail polish on her toes. Her perfume. Vanilla. A silver toe ring. The jingle of her earrings and necklaces when she moved. Her rapid breathing. The tap of her fingers on her steering wheel, drawing attention to her silver bracelets. Which made the total lack of nail polish and rings on her hands stand out.

"I'm fine." She didn't sound fine. She sounded agitated. Very agitated. Still, he caught the hint of an accent.

"No hurry." He shot for the whole approachable-normal-guy thing. Not well enough, apparently, because she was staring at him.

She stared up at him with big hazel eyes. No, more light green than hazel. Dark smudges beneath.

A slight crease formed between her brows as she looked him over, head to toe.

"But there is coffee inside," he offered. "Or water. And air-conditioning."

It took effort to lift her hands from the steering wheel, he could tell. But she did it. "Coffee would be nice," she murmured, grabbing the massive bag on the seat beside her and climbing—hurriedly— from the car. With a jingle of jewelry and a swish of skirts, she slammed the door so hard he winced.

Charley's ears pricked forward, glancing back and forth between them with interest.

"Is that her?" she asked, cautious.

"Who?" He understood then. "Sierra? No, ma'am. We'll go through some paperwork first, talk a little. Then, we'll see about getting you two together."

She frowned.

What had she expected? She'd pull into the parking lot, he'd bring Sierra out and put her in the car, and then they'd drive away? Nope. No way. The vetting process for a nonhandler or military family was more extensive. All of which was spelled out on the website and the paperwork she'd had to fill out and send in. But, since she was clearly battling with some sort of panic attack, he figured now wasn't the time to bring that up.

Instead, he made introductions. "This big guy is Charley. We're a team."

Charley faced the woman, cocked his head to one

side and wagged his tail in greeting. He was much better with people than Hayden was. So much so that, for a fleeting second, the woman smiled.

"Hayden Mitchell." He held out his hand. "You must be Dr. Vega?"

"Yes." That started the head shaking again. And her nose crinkled. It was oddly charming. And vulnerable. "I am, but, call me Elizabeth, please." Her handshake was firm—silky-soft against his work-toughened skin.

Feminine.

From her long dark hair to the flowing top and embroidered skirt she wore, Elizabeth Vega was undeniably feminine. Strikingly so. And those eyes. Soulful. Intense. And wounded. He might not be the most intuitive member of his family, but he knew all about internal wounds. Those could fester and cause more damage than the physical kind.

That's why she was here.

Not to have him staring, awkwardly, at her in the parking lot. She was pretty. No, more than pretty. Only a damn fool could miss that. He wasn't a fool. But, pretty or not, wounded or not, his job was to make sure Sierra was matched with the right person. The dog had done and seen things, been passed along too many times already—it was up to him to make sure this time, it was forever.

With what he hoped was a welcoming smile, he nodded toward the door. "This way."

* * *

Every nerve was firing distress. The sensation was so consuming it was hard to get her bearings. All this. The drive. The city. Locating the K-9 Placement Center just south of the air force base on the outskirts of San Antonio, Texas. Unfamiliar. Lovely land, ruggedly so. But no matter how lovely the view, from the rolling hills to the gorgeous man and his perky-eared dog, she couldn't shake the unease weighing down her chest. *Damn storm.* She'd been fine, excited even, until she'd hit the halfway mark of her trip and a thunderstorm turned the sky black and turned her insides into a jumpy, unsettled mess.

She followed Hayden Mitchell's broad back, breathing deep and concentrating on relaxing and reminding herself why she was here. *To get my life back.*

One teensy little thunderstorm wasn't going to undo the time she'd spent with her therapist. Her progress was remarkable, according to Dr. Margot Peeler, her therapist. Three months ago, she'd have been panicking over *everything*. From the new surroundings, unfamiliar floor plans, and not knowing where all the doors and windows and exits were to avoid getting trapped... Since she'd started seeing Dr. Peeler, she'd learned how to find a focal point, practice mindfulness and take deep breaths to cut off her spatial-related-attacks before they reached epic proportions.

Now if only I could apply the same techniques to thunderstorms... Dr. Peeler told her to be patient. There was no way to rush this—if it was to be truly successful. She shook her head.

Lizzie, stop! She could hear her grandmother's voice, loud and clear in her head. *You can do this. You are too strong, too fierce a woman to be ruled by fear.*

That's why she was here. A promise to Grammy.

She stood taller, straighter, thinking of her beloved grandmother. Diminutive in size, but mighty in spirit. Like Lizzie. Like she *had been*. Like she wanted, desperately, to be again.

It wasn't easy, but she was getting there. Today was proof of that.

"The traffic was horrible," she started. Talking was a good way to chase off her nerves. "All the construction. Lane's closing here, detours there. And so many rude people, honking and cutting in. And then a terrible storm." She swallowed hard. *Why mention the storm?* That wasn't going to help. She sighed, trying again. "I saw two accidents. Two. And you know what? People were slowing down to see the accident. Really slowing down, to get an eyeful. Of what? What is that?" She sucked in a deep breath. "What is wrong with people?"

Hayden Mitchell held the door open for her, one

eyebrow cocked up, a small smile on his face. "I often ask myself the same thing, ma'am."

Snap out of it, Lizzie. Focus on this. Him. The *ma'am.* His strong, rough hands. Big. Capable. Oddly reassuring.

Focusing on him was a way better option than thinking about the storm. He was handsome, especially now that he was smiling.

That smile helped her cross the threshold. Until she heard a rumble, far off in the distance. She came to a sudden stop—so sudden Hayden Mitchell plowed right into her.

"Sorry," he mumbled, stepping around her.

She should say something like, "No need to apologize" or "It was my fault." Because it was. But the words stuck and clogged her throat while she waited, listening closely. Maybe it had been a passing motorcycle? A jet? Anything that wasn't thunder? She swallowed, clutching her bag to her chest as she gave the small office a once-over.

If Mr. Mitchell was thrown by her beyond bizarre behavior, he didn't let on. "You drove up from Houston this morning?"

"Yes." She searched the open room for something solid to focus on. Hayden Mitchell was easy on the eyes but continuing to stare at him, and his very nice smile, wasn't exactly normal behavior. So, another focal point was needed. The room wasn't big. A desk on either side. Military K-9 posters on the wall. A clock hung on the middle of the back wall, ticking away the hour, and a door beneath it. Another way out, maybe. A large plastic potted plant in one corner of the room. Sterile. Unremarkable. "Not too long a trip, without the traffic." She cleared her throat and tried again. "I remember when I was little, taking long car trips. I loved them—the people and places. Now, it's different. Maybe it was because I wasn't driving? Back then, I would read or do Mad Libs or sing to whatever my grandmother had on the radio." She shrugged. *Breathe. Relax.* It wasn't thunder. All was well and she could stop freaking out. Her hold eased on her bag.

"You take cream or sugar in your coffee?" He crossed to the small table against the wall next to the plastic plant. A single-serving coffee maker sat waiting, a rack of brightly colored coffee pods beside it, and two plastic cups full of individual sweetener packets and creamers.

"I can manage." She followed, determined to show him just how normal she could be. Coffee was normal. Doing something would help. And occupy her hands. If she were lucky, he wouldn't notice how badly she was shaking. "Thank you." But a quick glance his way told her he did notice. And that he was watching her. Closely.

That was part of it, wasn't it? Making sure she

was *fit*, period. And not just to take care of a dog. It was to show her boss that she was able to resume her responsibilities at the college and in the classroom. How had her boss, Dr. Rivera, dean of fine arts, put it? It was vital that she take this time for her total recovery and health before the start of the semester. Meaning, she had to stop acting neurotic and get a handle on her nerves or her job was in jeopardy.

Her job. Something she'd worked hard to earn. Something she was good at.

Vega women weren't weak. Her great-grandmother, legend had it, outlived hurricanes, mudslides and three husbands before she passed at 101. Lizzie's grandmother raised five boys on her own and worked three jobs to support her family, and still had time to embroider all the church choir and ceremonial robes. Lizzie's mother had been no different. Her father's heart attack had forced her mother into the workplace, working nights, holidays and weekends, yet she had never missed a single one of Lizzie's school functions.

But, no, not Lizzie. One tiny, little, scary thing happens and she falls apart.

She slammed the empty creamer cup onto the small table, knocking the cup of sugar packets onto the floor and bringing her instantly back to the present.

The present, where Hayden Mitchell stood, arms crossed, watching her.

Perfect. Just perfect. "I'm fine." She knelt, scooping the packets back into the cup and setting it, carefully, back in its place. "Just fine." *Don't look at him. Don't do it.* She looked.

He nodded. Once. Studying her. No expression. Nothing.

She had no right to feel defensive but she couldn't help it. There was no doubt what he was doing. He was making judgments. Noting unusual behaviors. *I have plenty of those.* Still, getting defensive wasn't going to help. "It was a long drive."

Another nod.

The bubbling hiss of the coffeepot filled the strained silence between them. And ratcheted up her mounting agitation.

It was easier to stare at the coffee, slowly filling up the white ceramic cup. The dark fluid kept going, rising higher and higher—not stopping. The higher the coffee got, the harder it was to breathe. She hadn't found a focal point, she was too rattled. In that instant she was back there, in the dark, water rushing in on her as she tried to find a foothold in the muck with the sludge sucking her shoes from her feet.

"Dr. Vega?" A voice penetrated the fog in her brain.

The coffee kept going, nearing the top of the cup. Darker and thicker and inescapable.

"Elizabeth?" Stronger then.

Still, she couldn't move. Couldn't think. The coffee slowly stopped, the last few drops shaking the smooth surface and causing ripples.

Why couldn't she move?

Something wet pushed against her hand, causing her to jerk away—and snapping her back to reality. Charley, tail wagging and tongue lolling, stood at her side.

"Good boy." Hayden Mitchell's voice was soft and low.

Words clogged her throat. Should she apologize? Explain? And what explanation could she possibly have for being terrified of a cup of coffee? Or why she was shaking so badly she could barely stay upright.

"You should sit." There was no judgment, just concern.

"I'm fine." Her words were automatic. Defensive. And an obvious lie.

His sigh grabbed her attention. "Ma'am, I respectfully disagree. Please, sit down—before you fall down."

She almost argued. Almost. But she was shaking so much that her only option was to take the very solid, very warm arm he offered and hope he didn't immediately pack her back into her car and send her home, dogless, for such odd behavior. But she couldn't leave. She couldn't. *Try, Lizzie.* She drew in a deep breath. *I can do this.*

But if her viselike grip on his arm hadn't drawn suspicion, the fact that she'd pressed her face against the hard ball of his shoulder surely would. Here she was, groping a complete stranger, all but guaranteeing she wouldn't be leaving with a dog—or her dignity—intact.

Chapter Two

He wasn't trained for this. Action. Strategy. Hell, combat. No problem. Adrenaline could get you through most anything. And he'd been good at it, proudly following orders and rules to the letter. At least in combat, you knew to expect the unexpected. Civilian life? He thought he'd come home and life would slow down—maybe even get a little boring.

The joke was on him.

Of course, when he'd taken this contract position with the government, *this* scenario had never occurred to him. There was no contingency plan for how to deal with a fragile woman leaning into him, her face pressed to his shoulder, while she clung to his arm for dear life. And she was. Holding on. With no sign of stopping.

He could see her shirtfront pulse in time with the racing of her heart and hear the waver of each and every breath and knew, right or wrong, he'd let her hold on to him as long as she wanted. The fact that she smelled like lavender and was distractingly soft against him shouldn't even register—not right now. But it did.

"I'm so sorry." The words were muffled against his shoulder.

He awkwardly patted her back. "No apologies necessary." Explanations? Maybe. But he kept his mouth shut.

She shook her head but stayed as she was, face buried and holding on. "No? Are you saying this is a regular part of your day? None of this is…strange to you?"

He wasn't sure what to say to that. So far, this had never happened before. But it wasn't bothering him. "I'm not saying that. But some days are stranger than others."

Her laughter was a pleasant surprise. "I will not ask you where I fall on that spectrum." Her hands dropped and she stepped away, releasing her hold.

When her gaze met his, there was no dismissing the very real, very tangible jolt between them. Alive and electric and completely disarming. He didn't do disarming. Ever. And since he'd never experienced anything like that before, he wasn't sure what the hell to do. Just that he needed to do something. Say something. Instead of standing there staring. If she hadn't spun around to doctor the no-longer-threatening cup of coffee, he'd probably have kept right on staring at her.

As it was, he returned to his desk, sat down and flipped through the paperwork before him. He didn't fidget. Years of standing at attention ended that habit. And yet, here he was adjusting the stapler, aligning the pencils, rotating the pen holder and stacking the papers into a nice, neat pile.

"You said Charley is your team?" She carried her cup of coffee to his desk. He was glad to see her relatively calm smile as she sat in the chair opposite him. Yes, she glanced around her, taking in her surroundings—but that wasn't unusual. Not in his world, anyway. "You served together?"

"I trained him, trained a good portion of the dogs that come through Lackland Air Force Base. When his handler was KIA and Charley came back too wounded to serve, I asked to keep him."

With a yawn, Charley sprawled out across the concrete floor.

"He looks okay now." She slowly rotated the cup in her hands. "He can't go back?"

"He lost most of the vision in his left eye so he's retired." For a while they thought he'd lose his eye but Charley had been lucky. And since he'd been able to adopt Charley, he was damn lucky, too.

"You think he misses it?"

He glanced her way. "I don't know. I imagine it's hard for them after being trained so hard, so long, to just be a…dog." A smile surfaced. "But, as far as dog's go, I think he's got a damn good life. Charley and I live on my family ranch. Acres of rolling hills to roam, and mischief to find for a dog as curious as he is."

"Sounds nice." Those hazel-green eyes turned his way. "What about Sierra? That's her name?"

He sat back in his chair, trying to control his response to that look. And those eyes. Without much success. He cleared his throat. "Yes, it is. She was one of the last classes I trained. Sweet and smart. Eager to please." He shook his head. "Maybe too sweet for the job she did."

"Which was?" The cup kept spinning.

"Search and recovery." He ran a hand over his head. "If she and her handler got there on time, rescue."

The cup stopped spinning and those eyes widened. "Search and recover *people*?" The words were soft. "From…what?"

"Collapsed buildings, battlefields, wherever she was needed." He nodded. "She did good work. Important work. Her handler was a solid soldier who took excellent care of her."

"Where is her handler now?" Her gaze fell, staring into her cup.

"In action, with a new dog." He sat forward, resting his elbows on the desk. "Sierra got real sick—an upper respiratory and nasal infection—lost her sense of smell. Without that, she can't do her job so—"

"She's been fired?" Her gaze popped up and locked with his. The flash of grief and pain on her face took his breath away. "When do I get to meet her?"

"Dr. Vega—" He broke off when she scowled at him. "Elizabeth, Sierra needs stability. A loving home and a place she'll feel safe. Not for an hour or a week but forever."

Her nose wrinkled again and she blinked, rapidly. "I understand." The defiant tilt of her chin surprised him. So did the flash in her eyes. "What are you saying?"

What was he saying? He didn't know. Most of the time he got an instant sense about a person. But she was messing with that. What mattered was whether or not the person hoping to adopt would be good for the dog, not whether the dog would be good for the person. He knew Sierra's attentive nature and devotion would help this woman. But what did Elizabeth Vega have to offer Sierra?

"I came here fully aware of the commitment I was making, Mr. Mitchell. You have no idea how difficult that was. The drive, the trip, everything. Even coming here." The edge to her voice grew.

Since she brought it up. "Why?" He sat back in his chair.

"Why?" she repeated, instantly wary.

"Why was it difficult? Besides the traffic and the accidents and the rude drivers." He waited. "Or the thunderstorms?"

She stood, gripping her purse to her chest. "That's none of your business."

Charley stood up, instantly awake and alert.

"Ma'am, I have to disagree." He crossed his arms over his chest. Seeing her all fired up was fascinating. Better than timid and jumpy, that's for sure. "Taking care of Sierra is most assuredly my business. It's my job to know that she's being placed with the right person. I don't know enough about you to know whether or not that's you."

Her hands were fisted now, twisting in the embroidered bag she hugged. Her gaze shifted to the door and for a split second he thought she was going to walk out. But then she was staring at Charley and Charley was staring at her. She stood, silently communicating with his dog. There were times he thought his dog could read his mind—how else could he know what Hayden needed when he needed it? And right now, he was working his magic on Elizabeth Vega. When that tail started wagging, her posture slowly eased and she eventually faced him, smiling.

Seeing that smile did it again. The jolt. *Dammit.* The thing. The tightening in his chest. The knock to the gut. The whole "What the hell is happening?" sensation that seemed to grab him by the throat and shake him around. He tore his gaze from hers and stared at the pile of papers before him.

She sank back into her chair. "I will do my best to answer your questions."

Where did he start? Why she'd sat in her car for an hour this morning? What exactly was it about making a cup of coffee that terrified her to the point of a full-blown panic attack? And what the hell had happened to her to put that kind of fear in her eyes?

He'd been staring at the paper on his desk for a good three minutes. Even Charley was waiting for some sign from his teammate. Movement. A look. Some acknowledgment that she'd just made the colossal mistake of opening herself up for a slew of questions she didn't want to face—or answer.

Maybe it was wrong to cling to the idea Dr. Sai had planted, but nothing else had worked. Not when it came to storms, anyway. Both Dr. Peeler and Dr. Sai said companion and therapy dogs could do wonders when it came to panic attacks and, since the calming techniques she'd learned were unable to conquer the attacks brought on by storms, a therapy dog

was the next logical step. "I need a dog, Mr. Mitchell. But I understand Sierra is special." After hearing
what the dog had been through, she had greater respect for Hayden Mitchell's hesitation. "If she meets
me, likes me, maybe *she'll* decide to keep me?" She
tried to infuse some humor into her desperation. "If
she doesn't, I'll leave."

He leveled her with a hard look. Unflinchingly
long. Suspicious. Wary. Then resigned. "You're willing to stick around for a few days? So she can decide?"

A few days? Where would she stay? A hotel?
Her palms grew sweaty and hot so she pretended to
smooth her skirts. "If necessary."

He didn't hesitate. "It's necessary."

"Oh…well. Yes." She clasped her hands in her lap,
working through options. At least he wasn't sending
her home—not right away.

"Good." He stood, crossed to the door at the back
of the room. "Give me a minute."

She nodded. Today was a catastrophe. In her
mind, she'd imagined exactly how it would go. How
together and sane she'd act. Educated and totally
professional. And competent, of course. The dog
would run out, she'd instantly feel whole again, and
they'd ride home—happy and ready to return to a
normal life.

She'd always had an active imagination.

Instead, Hayden Mitchell thought she was unstable. Because that's exactly how she was acting. Stable people didn't have episodes in their car or freak out when making a cup of coffee or latch onto a total stranger. He had every right to be concerned about her ability to care for Sierra.

Poor Sierra. Doing the work she'd done, getting sick, losing her person and now…winding up with her? Maybe she should go—for the dog's sake.

"Poor Sierra," she murmured.

Charley's nails tapped on the stained concrete floor as he crossed to her and sat at her feet.

"I bet Mr. Mitchell could find someone better for Sierra," she said. Charley's tongue lolled out the side of his mouth in a doggy grin and he placed a paw on her foot. She laughed, offering her hand for his inspection. "Are you smiling at me?" He pushed his head under her hand and sat while she scratched behind his ear.

He had short, slick hair. Unlike Taffy.

Little yappy Taffy. How many nights had she trekked outside because Mrs. Lawrence, her elderly neighbor, had called in a panic over her escape-artist dog squeezing out and under the fence? Too many times to count. Lizzie would go, flashlight in hand, braving the mosquitoes and shaking a treat bag until the Taffy would appear—dirty and happy and ready to go home.

Lizzie hadn't seen them since the hurricane had torn their lives apart. Once Mrs. Lawrence had been released from the hospital, her son had moved her and Taffy in with him in Scottsdale, Arizona. They exchanged postcards—Mrs. Lawrence didn't believe in email—but there were times Lizzie missed scouring her neighborhood for the little white fluff ball and the inevitable thank-you basket of homemade fudge and cookies Mrs. Lawrence would deliver to her the next day.

Their little house sat vacant now, a hollow reminder of the nightmarish two-day ordeal she and Taffy had shared. Yet every time she saw it, she was back inside, trapped in the pantry, roof falling in and water rising and rising. Still, she'd held Taffy up, crooning nonsense the whole two days, hoping and praying for a miracle.

The click of the door handle announced Hayden Mitchell's return. But this time, he wasn't alone. A snow-white Labrador trotted behind him, ears and tail perked up.

Sierra was absolutely beautiful. Graceful.

Lizzie was instantly enchanted.

And bewildered. Now Sierra was real—flesh and blood and, possibly, her responsibility. Dr. Rivera had his doubts about her ability to take care of her responsibilities at her job. Clearly, Hayden Mitchell had doubts she'd be able to look after Sierra. Even Dr. Sai, the counselor the university had made available to all those struggling with the impact of the hurricane, suggested she take a sabbatical for the fall semester—until she was *coping better*. Dr. Peeler was helping with the coping. Now, with Sierra, she stood a chance of returning to her life and her job. *If* Sierra came home with her, that is. At this point, it was a pretty big *if.*

"This is Sierra." Hayden glanced at her. "Sierra, this is Elizabeth." He pointed at her and Sierra peeked her way, then trotted toward her, tail wagging.

Sierra's eyes were chocolate brown, satiny rich and surprisingly expressive. She reached Lizzie and immediately began sniffing her lap and hands, the strength of her nose sniffing similar to the thump-thump of a helicopter.

She laughed, setting her purse on his desk and holding her hands out for the dog.

Sierra's tail wagged harder, ears perking up and eyes on her face.

"Aren't you beautiful?" she whispered, her hand sliding along the dog's soft head. "She can't smell anything?"

"Maybe. Just not enough to do what she's trained to do." He squatted between Charley and Sierra. "Doesn't seem to bother her too much. How about we take them for a walk?"

"That sounds great."

It was the beginning of September, a little after ten in the morning, but the thermometer mounted to the side of the building read ninety-nine degrees.

"Guess summer is going to run long this year.

Too bad, it'd be nice to get a break from this heat," Hayden said. "You work at the university?"

She glanced at him. "I do, yes. But I'm taking some time for myself." She'd had to provide basic information on her adoption application. Things like address, character references, income—everything that proved she was a gainfully employed and functioning adult capable of dog ownership.

"By choice?"

She stole another look his way. "Mutual agreement."

His stern expression softened. "What does 'time for yourself' mean?"

"Taking care of myself." *Counseling.* "I'm not sure yet," she added. "Getting to know Sierra, I guess."

When she glanced at him, he was smiling, a small smile—nothing necessarily remarkable but it changed his entire demeanor. She really, really liked Hayden Mitchell's smile.

Charley and Sierra set off on a well-worn path leading away from the building and into a tree line, leaving them to follow. "They don't need a leash?" She watched the dogs trotting ahead.

"Not here. This place is a second home to them. The K-9 Center was built adjacent to the base so the dogs could still visit the training facility. Through the gate, there, and we're on base." He shook his head. "You can tell they know where we're going."

"Where are we going?" she asked.

"The course." He looked down at her. "Down the hill is the obstacle course they trained on. They like to run through it now, nose around and scent out the other dogs that have gone through. There's a running track too, to help them build up endurance with their handlers."

It quickly became apparent that she was having a hard time keeping up with Hayden's long stride. The man was well over six feet. She was just over five. Without saying a word, he slowed.

It was nice of him. Overall, he seemed like a nice guy. And when it came to these dogs, his heart was in the right place. He might be a little gruff. A little quiet. Slightly intimidating. And giant-sized. But he hadn't shooed her out of his office after she'd had a panic attack. His attempt at a joke—to make her feel better—had been kind.

"We'll have to cut this short." He pointed over-head. "Before that hits."

Overhead the clouds were rolling, shades of black and gray blotting out the sun and stealing any chance of reassuring Hayden that she was, in fact, a sane and rational person. "This is very bad," she whispered.

Chapter Three

It was like watching water freeze. From carefree movement and grace to painfully rigid and brittle. All it took was one look at the sky. The wind lifted her hair, made her bracelets and necklaces jingle, and the layers of her skirts twist and billow around her calves. But Elizabeth Vega was a statue. A beautiful, terrified statue.

"I need to go," she whispered, her lips barely moving.

"Now?" All Mark had said was Elizabeth Vega had been affected by the hurricane. Nothing more. While he understood the importance of doctor-patient confidentiality, he wanted to understand what was happening. Something *was* happening; he got that much. He whistled shrilly, and the sound of barking could be heard in the distance.

Charley and Sierra crested the hill at the same time the first big drops of rain started. It wasn't a heavy rain, more of a sprinkle. But the drops were big enough to feel. The dogs snapped at the drops, circling around each other and enjoying their moment of freedom.

But Elizabeth stood, staring up, rain pelting her face and shaking like a leaf.

"Come on," he murmured, using the same tone he used on his baby son when Weston was upset. He couldn't do the baby-talk thing; his vocal cords rebelled. But low and soft, almost coaxing, he could manage. It also came in handy in training—the voice he used when a dog or a handler got caught up in their head, too scared or disoriented to keep moving or remember their mission. It happened from time to time, normally with new recruits. "Let's go."

He, Charley and Sierra waited.

Nothing.

Because she wasn't *there*. The rain had triggered whatever this was and she was stuck in the middle of it. What she needed was a way out. He wiped his face and stepped forward, hesitated, then took her hand.

She blinked once. Twice. Then her fingers threaded with his. When she finally *saw* him, she gave him the saddest smile he'd ever seen. That smile… It damn near tore his heart out. The urge to protect kicked in something fierce. He needed to know what the hell he was protecting her from. With a shake of his head, he tucked her hand under his arm and led her back to the K-9 Placement Center office as fast as he could.

But she pulled away when they reached the porch, lingering there, beneath the awning—edging away from the door. He shoved aside the questions flooding his brain and gave her some space.

Who was he kidding? The space was for him. He was a little too tempted to offer her his shoulder again, to let her hold on to him until whatever this was passed again.

With a groan and a yawn, Charley flopped onto the concrete, staring into the rain, panting and content. Sierra sat looking pretty, ears perked up and brown eyes bouncing between him and Elizabeth.

Hayden couldn't look at Elizabeth, not yet. Or he'd end up reaching for her—he knew it.

He leaned against the railing, running a hand over his close-cropped hair to knock the water off. The clouds would break now and then, the rain coming in spurts—a few drops to a heavier downpour. If they were lucky, they'd have a good soaking rain, not just here but at his ranch forty miles north. The ground was so dry at the ranch it was cracking, and the idea and cost of hauling in water to fill the tanks would put them further in the hole.

One step at a time. No point worrying about what

might happen. He'd learned that on his first tour. Worry was a waste of time and energy.

Time.

He glanced at his watch. Almost eleven thirty. Dammit. His mother would give him an earful when he got home. Weston woke up howling. And that boy had lungs. He grinned. He loved his son. Everything about him was joy.

"I'm sorry." She sounded *almost* okay.

"For what?" He turned to face her. She wasn't any calmer now than when the first raindrop had fallen. Pressed against the side of the building. Eyeing her car, then the door to the office. She was gnawing on her lip so hard he worried she'd break the skin.

"Wasting your time." Her gaze wandered to Sierra, who instantly started wagging her tail. "I thought… I don't know what I thought. But this was *difficult*. And it probably shouldn't be. Not like this, anyway." There was that smile again, gutting him and pissing him off all at the same time. Who or what had done this to her? "I'm taking up your time. And her time. This was a bad idea."

Sierra was watching her closely.

"Nothing worth doing is easy, Elizabeth." Which was true. He felt helpless—watching as she wrapped her arms around her waist, hugging herself. He'd no business soothing her. *None.* Period. He crossed his arms and stayed put. The urge to comfort her was hard to resist but he had to.

"I know." Her voice broke. "Believe me, I know. But right now, nothing is easy." She stared at him. "You were there, you saw. The storms on the drive? That was all it took… I can't even make a cup of coffee without falling apart. It doesn't matter where I am. At home. Work. Total humiliation." She ran her hands up and down her arms. "The store." She was chewing on the inside of her lip again. "I just…panic. Even in my own bathtub." She broke off, covering her face. "I wound up sitting there, in cold water, for an hour—until the storm moved on."

He swallowed, wondering what had happened to haunt her like this. *Haunted* was the right word for it.

She pushed off the wall then, eyes wide. "I can't believe I'm telling you this. Honestly, I'm not *quite* this bad. Normally. Really." Her cheeks were red. "I wouldn't believe me, either. I'm sorry." She knelt in front of Sierra. "It was nice to meet you. I'm sorry I can't be your forever person."

Sierra's tail went wild and she stepped forward— but Elizabeth was already running through the rain to her car. She climbed inside as the sky opened up and pounded down. The lights on her little red car cut a direct path to the porch, where Sierra stood— barking and wagging her tail.

Today was a new low. Oh, so low. *Pathetic, Lizzie.*

"He didn't deserve that," she murmured, doing her best not to remember the look of pity and surprise on his face before she'd sprinted toward her car. Or Sierra's barking—that had tripped up her heart.

For one thing, the whole scene was ridiculously dramatic.

Her mother was dramatic. Her grandmother was over-the-top dramatic. She prided herself on being the only Vega who didn't have a flair for the dramatic. Expressive, yes. But that was different.

It was also a huge step back. She'd come so far, been so proud of herself… And she'd come all this way to wind up making an absolute fool of herself.

And what had she been thinking, unloading on poor Hayden Mitchell?

Yes, she'd shared with Dr. Sai and Dr. Peeler, but they were trained therapists, for crying out loud. Hayden Mitchell was not. He was a soldier. Ripped and fit, with ridiculously broad shoulders and an incredibly hard and surprisingly warm arm she'd clung to… She blew out a slow breath. Panic attack aside, meeting Hayden Mitchell, Charley and Sierra had been the highlight of her week. Month… Whatever. She'd ruined it, ruined her chances. She knew that. After *everything*, there was no way he'd let her adopt Sierra. That beautiful sweet girl.

Leaving had been her only option. She *was* going home. Alone. Rain or no rain.

It didn't matter that she was going thirty-five down the interstate. Or that people were honking and flying past her. It didn't matter that she was almost out of gas and totally turned around. It didn't matter that the rain was coming down so hard, she wasn't sure what was worse—her panic or her range of vision. But when the golden glow of a gas station sign signaled a reprieve from her self-imposed torture, she took the exit, pulled into the lot, found the highest spot to park and turned off the ignition.

Only then did she realize she didn't have her purse.

"Are you kidding me?" She slammed her hands on the steering wheel. "Really?"

No phone. No wallet. No help. *Come on, Lizzie.*

Not that there was anyone to call. She was in the middle of nowhere. Her family was hours away.

The knock on the window made her jump and, possibly, scream a little.

Hayden Mitchell was there, rain dripping off the brim of his cap. "Sorry. I followed you. The road's washed out ahead," he said loudly, over the roar of the rain.

All she could do was stare. He was here?

"Did you hear me?"

She nodded. "Wet," she mumbled.

"What?" he asked, cupping his ear to hear her.

"You're drenched." Which probably wasn't news to him since he was standing in the rain. She shook her head. "My purse. I left it in your office."

He ran a hand over his face, the corner of his mouth

kicking up. "Let's go back." He paused. "Wanna ride?"

She should say no. But her car would never make it there and back on what she had left in the tank. And, honestly, she was going to have to peel her fingers off the steering wheel as it was. "Please."

"Sorry, I don't have an umbrella." He waited for her to shrug before pulling open the door.

She ran to his truck, further amazed when he opened the door for her versus getting out of the rain himself.

"Hand up?" He helped her up into the cab of his large gray four-door truck and slammed the door.

She stared at him through the rain. She should be embarrassed. He'd followed her—meaning he'd been going way under the speed limit, too. Wonderful. Embarrassed or not, she was also relieved. And thankful. If he hadn't followed her... Well, she didn't want to think about that.

Once he was finally sitting next to her, he was soaked through.

"Do you have a towel?" she asked, turning to look in the back seat and finding Charley and Sierra sitting calmly. "Well, hello. Don't suppose there's a towel back there?" But her gaze snagged on the empty car seat strapped in place between the dogs. A car seat.

He had a baby?

He was a father.

Which meant he was definitely a husband.

It wasn't a shock, really. He was nice. And incredibly good-looking. Plus, the whole manners thing. Which reminded her. "You said something about the road being washed out?"

"You wouldn't have made it much farther." He nodded, stretching one long muscled arm over the back seat and pulling out an army-green T-shirt.

"Does that happen—" He was pulling off his shirt and whatever she'd been thinking of saying sort of faded from her brain.

As a sculptor, she found this was a body worth studying. He looked like he'd been carved from marble. Chiseled to perfection. Each muscle visible. Not scary big—impressive. Very impressive. As a woman... Well, yes, impressive. Appealing. And, apparently, distracting enough to forget the torture each raindrop caused her fragile nerves.

When she realized she was staring—and there was no denying she was obviously, no holds-barred, in-your-face staring—that was about the time he realized she was staring. A curious V formed between his brows and his crooked grin, the one she'd been admiring when he was standing outside her car window in the rain, appeared again.

If only if wasn't pouring rain and she wasn't a basket case and there wasn't an infant car seat in the back seat... What then? It didn't matter. This was reality.

"You're certainly fit," she mumbled. "I'm a sculptor. I sculpt things. People. You'd be…" *Stop. Don't say it. No.* "…an excellent model."

His brows rose and that grin grew wider. "I'll take that into consideration."

"No. Oh, no, I didn't mean for me." She was shaking her head. "I just meant…" *What? What do I mean?* She had no idea. Only that she had found a whole new level of mortification, right here, right now. "It was a compliment. Are we leaving? Now? After you put on your shirt?" Her cheeks were blazing.

"Yep." He tugged on the shirt. "I have to make a stop before we head back to the center first."

If it delayed her drive in the pouring rain, okay. "Of course."

"Good." He put the truck in Reverse, turned on a news radio station and began backing up. "If you need me to pull over, just let me know." No judgment. No teasing. Nothing. A statement. It was one of the sweetest things anyone had ever said to her.

"Thank you," she murmured, a lump in her throat.

The drive went pretty well. Except when she grabbed onto the door handle and forgot to breathe. Her eyes were pinched shut so tightly, she didn't realize Sierra had wedged her nose between the door and her seat's headrest until she felt her wet nose against her ear.

"She's worrying about you," he explained.

"Is she, Mr. Mitchell?"

"If I'm calling you Elizabeth, you're calling me Hayden." He was too focused on his driving to look at her, but the tightening of his expression tipped her off that something was wrong. "I have some bad news, Elizabeth."

"Okay?" Her hands tightened on the door handle. "Bad news as in we're about to wash off a bridge and plummet to our death?"

He laughed.

If it was bad *bad* news, he wouldn't laugh, right?

"That would be bad news." He risked a glance her way, tapping the radio console. "That new road closure? The one they just announced? That affects us. You're not going to be able to get home tonight. When it floods like this, we're cut off, though it should be clear tomorrow—if the rain lets up."

She hadn't been paying any attention to the radio. "Oh." Not the bad news she was expecting, but not good news. "Is there a hotel?"

He shook his head. "On the other side of the washed-out road. My family's place is big, plenty of room." He looked at her then. "And it will give you time with Sierra. If you still want that?"

Lizzie was in shock. "You mean it?" She reached back, sinking her fingers in Sierra's soft fur to offer a rub, only to be rewarded with a Labrador kiss. "Why, thank you."

"You're welcome," he said, that grin back, followed by a chuckle. "You were talking to the dog."

"No, no. Thank you, Hayden." She swallowed. "I mean it. You have no idea what your kindness means to me." It was too hard to look at him then. The poor guy didn't need her crying on him on top of everything else she'd put him through today. "And thank you for coming after me. In the rain. You sort of rescued me."

The muscle in his jaw tightened, but he didn't say anything.

Chapter Four

She had no way of knowing the rescue comment felt like a dig more than a compliment. Why would she? His ex-wife had accused him of having a rescue *complex*. And not just once, either. Karla had laid it out there, making sure he understood it wasn't a good thing.

But, growing up, his stepfather had given him no choice.

As the oldest, he'd had to look out for his two brothers. He always would. Not that either one necessarily appreciated it at the time. Hell, John—the youngest—still didn't appreciate it.

After Hayden had finished school, he'd immediately enlisted. Being a soldier was perfect for him: protection and defense. For years, he'd pretty much eaten, slept and breathed his job. He'd been damn good at it. He saw what needed to be done and he did it.

Today, well—maybe he *had* been on a rescue mission. He'd walked back inside the K-9 Placement Center, with the sky rumbling and the lightning crashing, and known what he had to do. He had to go after her. In the agitated state she was in, she shouldn't have been on the road. Then the radio had issued an alert, warning of the road closure, and he was glad he'd followed his instinct.

It wasn't hard to catch up to her. She was going twenty miles under the speed limit, her flashers on and her windshield wipers on high, slinging the water back over the roof of her tiny car and onto the hood of his truck. Finding her white-knuckled and panicking in the gas station parking lot hadn't been a surprise but the look on her face had triggered his protective side and he'd had no choice but to offer her shelter until the storm passed.

Hayden had never been so aware of every bump and pothole along the small farm-to-market road leading to his home as he was today. Because every time his truck bounced, every time his engine revved, every time he had to adjust the defrost setting to clear his windshield, Elizabeth Vega looked ready to leap out the window and into the pouring rain.

"You're from Houston?" he asked, doing his best to draw her into conversation again. Maybe he'd find just the right topic to distract her from the storm.

"Yes." She had her eyes pressed shut.

Okay—it hadn't exactly been an original question. Strike one.

"Born and grew up there?"

"Yes." She swallowed.

Yeah. As far as questions went, not much better. He sighed. Strike two.

"And you teach?"

"I'm a professor at University of Houston. Art, sculpting, pottery..." Her hand flew to the ceiling, bracing herself as they went down a slight dip in the road.

At least he'd gotten more than one word out of her. Enough to encourage him to ask, "How did you get into art?"

"I appreciate you trying to distract me from the storm, I really do. But I can't do my calming exercises and answer your questions." She took a deep breath.

As far as he could tell, the calming exercises were not working. If anything, she looked about ready to hyperventilate. And soon. But he held his peace and kept on driving, switching on the four-wheel drive once they crossed the cattle guard beneath the worn metal-and-stone gate leading to his home.

"Almost there," he murmured. Maybe knowing

they were nearing their destination would help with her calm.

Her hazel eyes popped open, her forehead creasing as she surveyed the wide-open fields of his home. "Where do you live? In the middle of nowhere?"

"Pretty much." He nodded. "This is prime horse and cattle territory. Goats and sheep, too. If you're so inclined, of course."

"I'll keep that in mind."

He would have laughed if a crash of thunder hadn't seen her covering her face with her hands.

"My great-grandmother traded her place in Castell for this property. It was less acreage but far more fertile soil. She'd grown up growing onions so she had to learn all about growing peaches and pecans." From the corner of his eye, he saw Elizabeth's body relax, her head angled toward him. He'd talk the whole way home if it stopped her from having a panic attack. "After she started making a little money on crops, she turned around and sunk it into livestock. She had a good eye and people started to take notice."

"What about your great-grandfather?" She was watching him then, interested.

"He got shot." Hayden shook his head. "There's a whole bunch of family lore and speculation on the who, what and why. The only thing we know for certain is, within a few days after his death, she'd traded property, packed up her kids in a wagon and headed here on her own. She was hardy stock."

"She sounds like an amazing woman." Elizabeth was studying him.

"That's putting it mildly." He chuckled. "*Stubborn* is another word. And it served her well." He couldn't remember a single story about his great-grandmother that didn't end with her getting her way. Through charm or sheer force of will, once she'd made up her mind—it was a done deal.

"Sounds like my grammy." There was a smile on her face.

If it wasn't for that smile, he probably would have managed to dodge the new dips the water was already cutting through the clay dirt roads. Once he hit them, her smile was a thing of the past. She was back to bracing herself against the ceiling, eyes squeezed tight, and far too pale. He corrected, hugging the right side of the road as they drove on.

The house came into view.

"There is it," he said, hoping he could coax her eyes open once more.

One eye opened, then the other. "You weren't kidding about living in the middle of nowhere." She glanced between him and the house. "So, you're a soldier and a rancher?"

He nodded. "Pretty much."

"And a home-finder for homeless dogs." She

peered into the back seat. "You two are very well behaved, by the way."

"They should be." He chuckled then. "The amount of time and energy I've invested in them. If they weren't, I'd lose all credibility." He shrugged. "Before I transitioned into the reserves, training the handlers and their dogs was my responsibility."

He pressed the electric gate opener and stopped, waiting for the cattle-proof fence to open wide enough for his truck. He pulled through, drove around the rear of the sprawling ranch house, opened the electric garage door and pulled his truck inside the cavernous shop his father had built.

Elizabeth Vega eyed the contents of the shop, looking almost as agitated as when they'd been bouncing down the dirt road leading to the main house.

"What's wrong?" He kept his voice low and even. "You all right?"

She nodded. "No." Her gaze bounced from the wall to the corner to the rack overhead. "Can we go inside?"

"Yep." He opened his door, called the dogs down and headed around to her side to open her door. She was already out, damn near huddling against the door leading into the house. "Go on in."

As soon as she opened the door, they could hear Weston. He wasn't just crying, he was full-out screaming.

"Is everything okay?" Elizabeth asked, following him inside.

"I'm not sure." He was already heading down the hall to his son's room. But Weston wasn't in his room. Or in the playroom. He was in his mother's room, in a playpen, holding himself up, screaming for all the world to hear him. "Mom?" he asked, concerned.

"In here, Hayden." His mother's voice was thick and rough. "Don't come in. I'm sick."

He scooped up Weston, who instantly stopped crying. "What can I do?" he asked.

"I'm hoping a hot bath and a nap will take care of it but…" She broke off, cleared her throat and tried again. "I can't seem to keep a thing in my stomach."

"I'm sorry, Mom." He sighed, giving his son a silly face and a wink. "I'll get Weston out of your hair. You get some rest. I'll come check on you later."

"Thank you, son." She groaned.

Hayden carried Weston down the hall and into the living area. "I brought you someone to meet, Weston."

Elizabeth stood in the middle of the living room, Sierra on one side and Charley on the other. All three of them were staring. Charley and Sierra lay on the floor, watching the rolling black clouds. But Elizabeth Vega was staring intently at the cuckoo clock his grandfather had made years before. So intently that she was completely unaware of their presence.

Which was good, because he needed a minute. Beneath her fragile exterior, she was strong. She might not believe that, but he did. At the first sign of the storm, she could have turned around and headed home. She hadn't. Was she struggling? Yes. And even though it'd be hard for him to stay impartial, he had to be. Elizabeth wasn't here for him to save. She was here to save herself. Once she realized that, nothing would stop her.

Lizzie traced the detailed carving on the clock face. Intricate. Delicate. Amazing. It was a work of art. And exactly the sort of thing she could use to help center herself. She took a deep breath. *Not thinking about the contents of the garage.* Saws, axes, metal sheets and what appeared to be the blade of some sort of large piece of farming equipment… nightmare-scenario stuff. *But perfectly acceptable things to have on a ranch.* She slowly exhaled. *Not that I want to have a picnic out there.* She smiled, taking another deep breath, and concentrated on easing the tension from her shoulders.

This was better.

The rain was still beating against the roof, but there'd been no thunder and lightning since they'd left the highway. Another breath in and out, her gaze following the eyelet notches that trimmed the clock. Her heart was no longer beating its way out of her chest. *Much better.* But her gaze bounced to the large panes in the rear French doors just long enough to offer her a less than nerve-soothing view. A creek. A rising creek. Not two hundred yards away from where she stood. *It's fine.* She swallowed. *Do not freak out.*

"You, um, want a seat or something?" Hayden Mitchell's voice was soft—probably because he was scared she'd overreact—again.

Be calm. Normal. I can do this. She turned and forced herself to face him... But the smiling baby in Hayden's arms was distractingly cute. "Who are you?" This was, without a doubt, the most precious baby she had ever seen.

"Weston," Hayden said, earning him an adoring smile from the baby. "Weston, this is Elizabeth."

She took a few steps forward. "Aren't you a handsome little guy?"

Weston was bashful. He pressed his face against Hayden's chest, but peeked at her—a toothless smile on his face.

The baby seemed okay now, but... "Is everything all right?"

"My mom is sick." He sighed. "She had him in a playpen. He was just letting the whole world know he objected." He bounced his son. "Truth is, he's started walking and he's faster than you'd think possible."

She had to smile then. "It's good to know your mind, Weston. Don't let anyone tell you different.

But always be nice to your grandmother. Especially when she's sick."

Hayden's laugh was deep and rich and just enough to catch her full attention.

His sandy-brown hair was the standard close-cropped military haircut. His eyes were a light brown. His features… Well, his chest wasn't the only thing worth sculpting. Not that she'd say so— this time. The fact that he was holding an adorable baby didn't hurt. "How old is he?" she asked, tearing her gaze away from the father to look at the son. *And where is the baby's mother?*

"Almost a year." Hayden shook his head. "Time flies."

"And walking? I bet you keep your daddy busy, don't you?" She tickled the bottom of Weston's sock-covered foot.

"He does. Believe me." Hayden nodded. "It's lunchtime for this one." He bounced his arm, making Weston giggle. "Are you hungry, Elizabeth?"

"It's Lizzie, actually." It's what her friends called her. After all he'd done for her today, Hayden Mitchell had proved he was friendworthy. "Um…" Food? She'd skipped breakfast because she'd been so anxious to get on the road. Now that he'd mentioned food, she realized just how empty her stomach was. "Yes. Please."

Weston's coos were turning a little more insistent. "I'm assuming you're not into strained peas or chicken and pears?" Hayden asked, carrying Weston across the room.

"No. Thank you." She lingered, staring around the inside of the house. The quick look she'd taken—before fixing all of her attention on the cuckoo clock—revealed an open-concept kitchen–dining room–family room. A nice home. Very ranchy. Lots of space—

"The front door is there." Hayden was at her side, pointing. "Large picture windows on either side. Another one there, in the hallway leading back to the bedrooms. Behind us are the French doors."

She stared up at him. He was giving her escape route options as if it was the most normal welcome-to-my-home sort of greeting.

"Just so you know, there's a window in every room. They're all latched, but easy enough to open." He nodded. "Peanut butter or turkey?" he asked, his light brown eyes meeting hers.

Her heart was still thumping along but it was for an entirely different reason now. She didn't want to think about what, exactly, made him feel the need to list off all of his home's escape routes. A face? A noise? *My overall cat-scared-of-its-own-shadow jumpiness all day so far?* Whatever the reason, he was being incredibly sweet. And patient.

His gaze swept over her face, slowly, carefully—lingering just long enough to make her chest turn warm and heavy. "Elizabeth?" He cleared his throat.

"Lizzie? Peanut butter or turkey?" A slow smile spread across his face.

The smile. The sweetness. And the baby. Plus the whole gorgeous-man thing. Hayden Mitchell wasn't something she'd expected when she set out this morning. Not that anything had gone the way she'd expected. "Peanut butter."

"You hear that, Weston?" He carried his son to the high chair next to a large wooden chair, moving with surprising efficiency and grace. "The lady wants peanut butter. Jelly?"

"None for me." She took a deep breath. "Hayden, I can make sandwiches and you can feed Weston. If you're okay with that?"

"I *am* okay with that." He nodded, buckling his son in. "And I appreciate it. The pantry is that way."

"Pantry?" She'd spent the last four months getting over her fear of pantries… Which was one of the more pathetic thoughts she'd ever had. She nodded. "Can do." And she could. And would. Like a 100 percent fully functional human being. She made a silly face at Weston, who was giving her a shy smile—followed by a giggle.

"Hold up. I'll get it." He ruffled the light hair on top of his son's head. "Flirt." He laughed when Weston garbled something, then nodded. "I thought so." He looked her way. "Can you sit with Weston?"

They were both watching her. She wasn't sure which she preferred: Weston's wide, toothless grin or *whatever* that look was on Hayden Mitchell's way-too-handsome face. "Sure." She sat beside Weston. "Hi, Weston."

Weston smiled, slapping his little palm on the tray.

"I agree." She nodded. "I like making noise, too." She tapped on the table.

He giggled, slapping a little harder this time.

"Oh, you're so strong." She smiled. "And so proud of yourself." She tickled his foot again.

"Do you have children?" Hayden asked, placing a loaf of bread, a jar of crunchy peanut butter, grape jelly and two jars of baby food on the table.

She stood, taking the knife and plates he offered and moving aside so Hayden could take his spot. "Many nieces and nephews." She shrugged. "I think I'm the only still-single person left in my family." She paused, thinking about it. "I am." That was not at all embarrassing to share with someone she'd just met. Especially this big, handsome man with gentle eyes who was probably not in the least surprised to hear she was single. "And you? Is Weston your only child?" She placed two pieces of bread on each plate and closed off the bread bag.

"One and only." Hayden nodded, the muscle in his jaw clenching briefly.

"Will his mother be joining us?" she asked, spreading peanut butter.

"No. Weston's mother and I are divorced."

She paused, watching Hayden put a bib on his son, then sit. "Oh." Weston was so young.

Hayden placed some whole-grain cereal onto Weston's high chair tray. "We get on just fine, don't we? I haven't heard you complain." He chuckled as his son jabbered away, then grinned. "You've got a little something right there." Hayden wiped crumbs from the baby's cheek.

Lizzie watched the exchange, hard-pressed not to smile. Little Weston looked at his father like he was the moon and stars and everything else. And Hayden... Well, Hayden was clearly smitten with his adorable son. She added grape jelly to one of the sandwiches, cut it in half and slid the plate across the table to Hayden.

"Triangle?" Hayden eyed the sandwich.

Lizzie looked at her plate, then his. "It would seem so. Does that have some sort of huge significance?"

"Just making an observation." He shrugged, glancing her way. "I'm a triangle man myself." He offered Weston a bite of his sandwich. "Charley." His tone was stern, waving a finger at the dog sitting beside the back door. "He's figured out how to open the back door—uses his nose to work the door handle." He sighed. "A trick I taught him before this little guy came into the picture."

Charley whined but lay on the floor, all repentance.

Lizzie was smiling as she took a bite of her sandwich, enjoying the faces Hayden made at his son, enjoying little Weston's happy giggles and coos. She glanced down to find Sierra lying at her feet, her soft doggy snores reaching her.

If only the rain would stop...

While Hayden cleaned up Weston, she put the jelly back in the refrigerator and carried the bread and peanut butter toward the pantry. She stood there, peering inside. It was bigger than Mrs. Lawrence's pantry. The shelves were deeper, for one thing. But it was still a pantry. No windows. No escape.

It's a pantry. She drew in a deep breath, pulled the door wide, turned on the light and stepped inside... At the same time thunder crashed and the whole house seemed to shake beneath her feet.

Chapter Five

Hayden unclipped Weston from his high chair. "All done?" He lifted Weston and bounced his son as another clap of thunder shook the house. Weston startled. "I know, that one was a doozy." His tone was soft and low.

Weston gurgled in response, rubbing his eyes with little fists. "Da, nigh?"

"I like to take a nap after I eat, too." Hayden nodded, turning. "Where did Lizzie go? Hmm? Do you see her?"

Weston gurgled some more, babbling and patting Hayden's chest.

He frowned, glancing around the kitchen. The

peanut butter and bread weren't on the table. Meaning she was putting them away? Another thunder strike. He'd seen her face. He'd watched her reactions. Rain. Thunder. Storms. All the cause of Lizzie's panic attacks. And a hell of a lot of fear. He marched across the kitchen, a sense of urgency building with each step.

"Lizzie?"

She jumped, shoving the jar of peanut butter and the loaf of bread onto the nearest shelf before hurrying out of the pantry, clicking off the light and closing the door. She sort of collapsed against it, breathing hard and wide-eyed. "Put the peanut butter away." She took a deep breath. "Bread, too."

The way she looked—relieved and a little proud—was…sweet. And heartbreaking. "I appreciate your help."

A clap of thunder had her pressing her eyes shut. She sucked in a deep breath and nodded, then blew it out slowly, unsteadily.

It took effort not to ask any of the questions cycling through his brain. Experience had taught him that the only way to effectively deal with a situation was through thorough data analysis. Not that she'd asked for his help. But the instinct was there, ready and willing to do so.

Maybe Karla was right. He was already working through ways to rescue Lizzie. She hadn't asked for his help. But was wanting to help someone a bad thing?

Weston yawned and drooped against his chest. "I think he's ready for his afternoon nap." He stared down at his boy, his small head resting on his chest. "Looks like he might already be halfway there."

Her hazel eyes focused on his son. "His little eyes are definitely getting heavy-lidded."

"Then I'll put him to bed." He paused, noting the instantaneous tightening of her posture. Rigid. Braced. Another clap of thunder and she was hugging herself, her skirts and jewelry jingling—the happy chime at odds with the thundering outside.

"You should come?" He paused, watching the color drain from her cheeks as a series of thunderclaps rent the air. "I'll show you where you're staying tonight."

"Oh." She nodded, her hands flexing against her layered skirts. "Yes."

"Good." He led them across the great room.

They were halfway down the hall when he heard her say softly, "It's a lovely home."

While the bare bones of his family home remained the same, his mother and stepfather had made some changes while he'd been in the service. Mostly, knocking down the walls that separated the kitchen, dining and living room. His first visit home after the renovation, he hadn't been a fan. But now, with Weston, he appreciated the openness. When his boy was wiggling and pushing his way across the floor, Hayden could keep an eye on him pretty much wherever his boy got to. Of course, that was before he'd learned the truth about his stepfather. It would take time to get the ranch back on track. Finding out about the total neglect of the property's financial state had been a shock. And these renovations, nice as they were, had only added to the debt. "Thank you. It's comfortable."

He pushed open the door to Weston's nursery, changed his son's diaper as quickly as possible—resulting in some mild fussing—then walked him back and forth, an extra bounce in his step, while he patted his son's back.

Lizzie stood in the doorway, her gaze jumping from him to the large picture window covered with thick, red bandanna-print drapes. *Stood* wasn't right. More like half leaned, half propped herself in the door frame. Even in the gloom of his son's large star-shaped nightlight, he saw how round her eyes were.

A more solid thump started against the ceiling. Alternating fast and light and slow and heavy. The sound was so bracing, he was surprised Weston didn't stir. Thankfully, he didn't. He carefully placed his son in his crib and crept from the boy's room and back into the hall.

"Hail?" Lizzie asked, her hand catching his forearm. Her touch ice-cold.

"Good thing we're inside." He stared down at her, watching her mouth. Was she counting?

Other than her nod, she didn't move.

"And that we parked in the shed." He took her hand, like it was the most casual thing in the world, and led her back down the hall and into the great room. "Want some coffee? Tea?"

She nodded, unaware or content to keep holding his hand. Even after they'd taken a seat on one of the large, overstuffed couches near the old wood-burning stove, she held on. But once they were seated, Sierra trotted their way, tail wagging, to sit in front of Elizabeth. It was enough to earn a smile from her—and for her to let go of him.

He watched the exchange. Sierra leaned into Lizzie's hand, making that little dog-groan of appreciation that always made him smile. Sierra was curious about Lizzie. Could be, the dog had already picked up on the woman's internal struggle. Not like it was all that hard to pick up on.

"I'm going to make some coffee." He pushed off the couch, taking care not to interrupt the woman-to-dog bonding happening, and set about making a full pot of coffee.

He took a look out the windows lining the back wall of the house. Lightning rippled across the sky— thunder following close behind. And the hail just kept on falling.

In front of the back door, Charley was sprawled

out. After one especially hard crack of thunder, the dog stretched, yawned and rolled onto his back. Hayden grinned. *Guess there's nothing to worry about, then.* If there was, Charley would be on alert.

A little storm, okay a hell of a storm, was a good thing in the long run. The drought had lasted long enough to result in a three-county-wide burn ban. One spark could set off the sort of chain reaction that could bankrupt a farming or ranching family. Something they might already be facing.

This rain would help. For a while, anyway.

While the coffee brewed, he did a mental checklist of their equipment, hoping like hell everything was where it should be. Hail damage could be costly— insurance or no insurance.

"You like that?" Elizabeth's voice was soft, soothing.

He glanced her way and paused, smiling.

Sierra had flopped back on her side, offering Elizabeth her creamy-soft stomach for a good old tummy rub. Elizabeth, sitting on the floor beside the dog, was all too happy to oblige. It was a heartening sight. It looked like Dr. Sai was right. Maybe all Elizabeth Vega needed was a companion animal—someone to distract and calm her when her tension levels were too much.

Sierra rolled over the other way, her long back pressed against Elizabeth's leg, and rested her head on her paws. Elizabeth lay her hand on the dog's back, her other hand tucking the fall of long black curls behind her ear. Her earring was long and dangly, spinning against the column of her neck.

He found himself staring at her earring—who the hell was he kidding?—her neck, for a hell of a lot longer than necessary.

There was something about the slide of bracelets along her arm, the soft jingle sound when she moved, and the curve of her cheek as she stared down at Sierra that held him transfixed. She was pretty, there was no denying that, but there was more to it than that.

I need to get out more.

He pulled out two coffee mugs and closed the cabinet with a little too much force. The resulting thud had Elizabeth, Sierra and Charley all looking at him with varying degrees of surprise. Well, Charley looked irritated. That dog loved to nap.

"Sorry." He hoped his apology smile was sufficient.

For the dogs, yes. They both resumed their prone positions. But Elizabeth's attention had wandered from Sierra to the window and the storm outside.

He poured the coffee and carried the mugs into the great room. Instead of sitting on the couch, he sat on the floor next to her—stretching his long legs out in front of him and leaning back against the couch. Mug outstretched, he waited for her to take it.

* * *

The thunder seemed farther away now. It had been a few minutes since lightning had split the sky. Even the hail and rain seemed to have eased up. Hopefully, this would be over soon. Hopefully, she was done having panic attacks and making a fool of herself.

She'd held his hand. *His hand.* This poor man had endured her episode in his office, driven through the rain to get her, brought her to his home—where she'd proceeded to have another episode and hold his hand… She should apologize. It seemed like so many of her conversations included them. Start, finish or peppered all throughout. She was an expert apology-maker. Hayden Mitchell deserved both an apology and a heartfelt thank-you.

The sudden movement from the corner of her eye had her turning, her heart instantly beating its way up and into her throat. Until she realized it was just Hayden.

Hayden, on the floor, at her side, holding out a cup of coffee. Something about him on the floor only reminded her of how big he was. Big and manly and sweet and on the floor holding out a cup of coffee like today was any old day.

A really, really *heartfelt apology.* "You didn't have to do that." But she took the mug, absorbing the warmth of the Texas stoneware into her palms.

Those light brown eyes of his were watching her,

again. Instead of being unsettled or annoyed, she felt…well, the opposite of annoyed.

The corner of his mouth kicked up. "You're welcome." He sipped his coffee.

"Thank you." She blew on the hot surface of the liquid, his gaze meeting—holding—hers. "Something about a mug. Holding it is therapeutic? The warmth…" *Well, that was insightful.* Her point had been? She'd had one, until she'd started to notice the slight lines around his eyes. The deeper brown and gold tones in his irises. A faint scar along the left side of his chin. He was truly, disarmingly masculine. *Handsome* wasn't quite right. She swallowed, realizing her assessment had gone for *far* too long.

"What?" he asked.

"What?" she repeated, horrified that, once again, she'd been caught staring.

"What's the smile for?" He turned to face her, resting his elbow on the cushion behind him.

She'd been smiling? Staring and smiling. *Wonderful.* "Um…" She took a sip of coffee. "I was thinking about the importance of first impressions." She took another sip, avoiding his gaze and the eyes and the scar and the…hotness. "And how I can only imagine the one I've made on you. Honestly, I'm surprised you're okay with me being here—in your home."

His gaze narrowed. "It seemed like the right thing to do at the time."

She had to look at him then, really *see* him. "It

did?" Because it was obvious she needed help. She was getting it. And, even though it didn't always feel like it, she was better… "I'm normally not this bad. I know you have no reason to believe me—"

"The storm." He nodded. "I get it."

I doubt that. But she only nodded.

"How long?" he asked.

There was no need for clarification. "Four months—give or take a few days." The hurricane season had been early and terrifying this year. Considering there was a credible threat through November, there was a very real chance it could happen again. Not being trapped with Taffy… But another hurricane.

This one, Hurricane Donald, had hit hard and early. No one had expected it to come so far inland. But it had. Parts of Houston were relatively untouched. Others were decimated.

"As far as first impressions go…" He broke off, considering his coffee for a moment. "It's definitely been memorable." It was said without inflection—leaving his words wide open to interpretation.

She was torn between humiliation and anger when he finally met her gaze and she felt that odd current between them. Odd because she'd just met the man. Odd or not, it was strong enough to derail her anger and humiliation and leave only… What? What was *this*?

This was her brain trying to come up with an alternative focus from the storm. It had nothing to do with the fact that she was outrageously attracted to this man. That made sense. *Sure, it did.* Bottom line, he was handsome—*fine, hot*—and she was in a super-needy spot and they were here, alone, on his far-removed ranch with nothing to do but drink coffee and stare at each other. At this point, she felt confident she'd fulfilled, possibly exceeded, an acceptable quota of staring.

"Looks like it's letting up." He nodded to the back door. "In ten minutes, we could have blue skies and sunshine."

"Or tornadoes and flash floods." She shrugged.

He glanced her way, laughing. "I suppose that's possible. It is Texas, after all."

Sierra lifted her head, stared between the two of them and rested her chin on Elizabeth's lap.

"Sorry, Sierra," she whispered, running her hand down the dog's back with long, slow strokes.

Sierra's chocolate brown eyes settled on her face.

"I hope that look means you forgive us," she whispered, her hand never stopping.

The dog's eyelids drooped shut, her breathing deep and even, and her full weight easing against Elizabeth. The thing was, she didn't know who was benefiting more. Her? Or Sierra? There was something cathartic about the dog's weight, something soothing about the slide of her fur beneath her palm.

"She's taken with you." Hayden placed his empty mug on the floor between them.

"Is she?" Elizabeth asked, watching the dog's face twitch. "Do they dream? Dogs, I mean? She looks like she's dreaming."

"They do." He paused, drawing her attention back up to the handsome face she was not going to stare at. "I wonder sometimes if a canine veteran dreams like their handlers. I mean, they are veterans, too. They've been in the thick of it, right along with their handlers." He shook his head. "I'd like to think they dream about going on a long run or eating a steak or napping on their favorite human."

Elizabeth stared down at Sierra, considering Hayden's words. "I like the sound of that last bit better." Her hand moved slower now, coming to rest on Sierra's back. "Steaks and no fences and endless bouncy balls to chase."

He nodded, that crooked grin back.

A silence settled. The sound of raindrops grew further and further apart and, while the sun didn't break through the clouds, there was no foundation-shaking thunder. As far as she was concerned, it was a step in the right direction.

"Is there someone you need to call?" Hayden asked. "Someone who might be expecting you home?"

"No." Her last serious boyfriend, an economics professor on campus, was now married and expecting kid number two. Meaning it had been years since she'd had a serious relationship. While she was still friendly with her ex, she wouldn't call him to inform of her whereabouts.

And Grammy was staying with one of her cousins in Wichita Falls. She tended to move from house to house now, staying a few months here, a few months there. Since there was family all across the state, it was her way of keeping up with her children and grandchildren. She liked that, staying connected. No fuss, no frills, just being part of the family while she was there. She'd finished up a lovely visit at Lizzie's house only a few weeks before the hurricane hit.

Thankfully.

Grammy had no idea Lizzie was here—or how significantly she was still struggling with the aftereffects of the storm. With any luck, she'd never know.

"Should you check on your mother?" she asked. "Make sure she's staying hydrated?" She swallowed. "If you're sitting here because of me… Well, Sierra and I are okay."

He studied her for a minute, then Sierra. "Okay." He pushed off the floor and stood. "Done with your coffee?"

She'd barely finished half her cup but she handed it up to him, anyway. "Probably shouldn't drink any more. You might not have noticed, but I'm a little wound up without adding more caffeine to the mix." She smiled, trying to make light of the whole beyond-bizarre situation they were in.

He nodded, taking her mug. "You're wound up?" His crooked grin was a thing of beauty.

She hadn't planned on watching him walk to the kitchen. Nope, she'd planned on staring out the back window to make sure the rain had, in fact, stopped. But it was pointless to resist the pull. At least now he wasn't aware of her ogling. And she was totally ogling.

His T-shirt hugged broad shoulders. *Very* broad. His arms resembled the marble she worked with occasionally. Not cold, but hard and commanding and full of promise...

Way to get carried away.

She wasn't going to start cataloging the impressive curve of his rear. Chances were it was just as rock hard as the rest of him. With a sort-of silent squeak, she tore her gaze away before he caught her—again—and glanced out the back doors.

The rain was picking up. Not the same assault-like-rain from before, but rain nonetheless.

"I caught a peek of the creek behind your house." Her fingers slid through the thicker fur at Sierra's neck. "It looked rather..." *Full. High. Fast. Rising. Dangerous. Bad.* She went with, "Close."

"It won't crest those hills, if that's what you're worrying about." He glanced her way.

"How do you know?" Had she really asked that? *I sound like a petulant child.*

She sighed.

"Well, my family has lived here for generations and it never has." He shrugged. "I'm sorry, Lizzie, that's about the only guarantee I can give you." He filled a glass with water. "I'll be back." He seemed to hesitate.

"I'm fine." She waved her hand at him. "Really. I am." It was only after he'd left the room that she realized she was, in fact fine. Even though she was in a strange place, with strange people, in the middle of a storm, she was fine. Another realization, one equally surprising, was how much she liked it when Hayden said her name.

Chapter Six

"Mom?" He rapped on the bedroom door with his knuckles. "I brought you some water." Because Lizzie was thoughtful. He felt like an ass for not thinking of it himself.

"You are a dear." The words were a croak. "You can come in, but beware the chemical smell. I've been spraying and wiping—I don't want Weston catching this."

The scent of disinfectant was so strong his eyes started to water. "Wow." He coughed. "No fear of that. How are you breathing in here?" He coughed again, tasting the bite of the cleaner on his tongue. "Seriously, Mom, you're going to asphyxiate yourself."

From the looks of it, she'd barely managed to drag herself into bed—her feet dangling off the edge and her hand still clutching what had to be a near empty can of antibacterial spray. He placed the water glass on the bedside table. "Did you take any pain reliever?"

"I haven't put a thing in my mouth for the last two hours." Her words were muffled against the comforter she was lying on top of. "Not that pain reliever will do anything for this nausea. For now, I'm content to not move for a while."

"Can I do anything?" She did look pretty green.

"No." She was breathing slowly. "I think the only option I have is for this to run its course. And for you and Weston to stay far, far away from me."

"Will do." He paused. "We have company. For all I know, she won't be here when you're up and about but, on the off chance you make a miraculous recovery, I didn't want you to be surprised."

"Company?" His mother turned her head, ever so slowly, so that one eye met his. "She?"

"It's work." He shook his head. "Storm came in, stranded her here. Couldn't exactly leave her on her own."

"Of course not." His mother's eye closed. "I'm sorry I can't cook for her."

Even on her sickbed, she was worrying about being a good hostess. "Mom, I feel confident she's not going to hold it against you."

"Promise me you won't feed her peanut butter sandwiches, Hayden. Promise me you'll cook her a proper meal—like I've taught you."

He decided not to mention the peanut butter sandwiches they'd already enjoyed for lunch. "I'll take care of it, Mom. You take care of yourself."

She lifted a shaky thumbs-up, moaned and let her arm drop back to the bed.

"And don't spray any more of that." He sighed. "Or you'll do permanent lung damage."

She mumbled something but he couldn't quite make it out.

"What?" he asked, heading toward the door.

"The sheets in the guest room are clean," she managed.

"I got it, Mom. Rest, please. I love you." He pulled her door closed behind him and headed back down the hall. A quick glance told him Weston was still snoozing, so he headed back into the great room. "My mother wants me—" But he stopped cold.

Lizzie Vega had dozed off, her hand still resting on Sierra's back. Sierra had curled around Lizzie, the dog's soft snore echoing in the mostly quiet room. If he didn't know better, he'd think the two of them were already deeply connected. Then again, with dogs like Sierra, it didn't take much. He'd rarely met a dog with such solid support instincts. It's like Sierra had taken one look at Elizabeth and decided to help her.

That was the difference between people and dogs. Dogs loved unconditionally, selflessly and were unfailingly loyal. He knew more than a handful of people who could take a lesson from their canine brethren—including his ex-wife.

He ran a hand over his head, struck by how peaceful Lizzie and Sierra looked. If the damn storm would break, she might be able to enjoy her time here tonight. One thing was certain—rain or no rain, there was no way they'd be getting Lizzie back to her car today. If it kept raining like this, chances were she'd be stuck here longer.

He was surprisingly okay with that.

Lizzie had piqued his interest. It wasn't just about Sierra. Not now. He'd met a lot of broken people in his time. Not just physically injured, but emotionally, too. He knew that most times the invisible wounds were the hardest to heal. There was usually a straightforward path to physical healing. But mental wounds weren't as black-and-white as he liked life to be.

Maybe being stuck out here wasn't the worst thing for Lizzie. There was no place to go, no time schedule to keep and—minus Weston's occasional fusses—she'd have plenty of peace to focus on herself. And Sierra. Hopefully, she'd come around to seeing the silver lining to her current predicament.

He turned on the television, muted, to keep up with the roadway and weather conditions and went in search of his laptop. While he was home, he might as well read through any new canine adoption applications and check his email.

First up were a series of emails from Bobby Doherty with a growing list of repairs they'd need to tackle once the rain stopped. Bobby, their ranch foreman, was good at his job—even if he wasn't good at technology. The man meant well but he tended to send multiple one-line to-do items versus making one email with the entire list. Hayden had learned to sit, legal pad in hand, and write them all down when it happened—so nothing got lost in the email string. Once he'd jotted down Bobby's list, he moved on.

A couple of bills from the feed store and a farrier bill for last month's visit. A few hits from several breeders with available bulls—complete with rates and dates available.

But his gaze fell to an email from his youngest brother, John. Emails from his little brother were few and far between. Normally, they were brief status updates—or as John put it, "letting you and Mom know I'm still alive" emails. John had no idea how much his emails meant.

He and John had a prickly relationship—that's how his mother described it. The truth was, John resented Hayden's attempt to parent and protect him from their stepfather. When their mother married Ed Simmons, the man had been sweet-talking, easy-smiling, quick to promise and easy on the eyes. It hadn't taken Hayden long to figure out the man was a con artist. For a while, John had seen only the Ed Simmons their mother had fallen head over heels for. Hayden and Kyle—the middle Mitchell brother—had solid memories of their father but John was a good deal younger than them. And Ed? Well, Ed had done his best to mold John in his image—taking the time to make John feel special. Until something happened that made John realize Ed was the last man he'd want for a role model.

Something John refused to tell him, or Kyle, about.

It didn't matter that he and Kyle had tried, time and again, to warn their younger brother about Ed Simmons's true nature. John had to figure it out for himself—a philosophy that had applied to every aspect of his life since. John was too proud and too stubborn to listen to what anyone else had to say. Which made his little brother's military career… *interesting*.

Hayden opened the email—then pinched the bridge of his nose. It was short and to the point, the way John always communicated with him. Bottom line, John's temper had, once again, got the best of him. He had been censured for instigating a fistfight. Again. But, this time, he'd been told this was his last chance. If John slipped up again, he'd face more serious consequences.

What troubled Hayden most wasn't the fighting,

it was John's lack of concern. His brother tended to attack things from the "Is that a challenge?" sort of angle. It had been exhausting as an older sibling. He could only imagine how worn out John's commanding officers had to be.

He opened a reply window and spent the next ten minutes writing and erasing potential responses. His brother rarely emailed so, when he did, Hayden tended to reply in as neutral tone as possible. The last thing he wanted was to lose contact with his brother altogether. Difficult or not, he was protective of the relationships he had with his brothers. So even if he wanted to rip into his little brother, to tell him to get his shit together, and to start being the man he could be, Hayden didn't. Instead, he told John to behave, gave him a rundown on the ranch, mentioned their mom was sick and that Weston took his first wobbly steps. He read over it again. And again. Then hit Send.

Placing his computer on a leather footstool, he stood and headed into the kitchen for another cup of coffee. His attention wandered from the still-falling rain to the television with the weather advisory alert scrolling across the bottom of the screen.

Shit.

Just as he suspected. Most of the farm-to-market and major roads leading to and around the ranch were now closed.

They'd be fine. If worse came to worst and they

lost power, they had a backup generator. And, since his mother preferred making big monthlong shops, they had plenty of food to last through the few days they'd likely be stranded.

He picked up the phone and called the owner of the Quik N' Go gas station, Walt Guinther. Since Lizzie's car wasn't going anywhere, he'd ask his old friend to keep an eye on it. Walt agreed, told him to be safe and hung up.

To be honest, the weather was doing him a favor. When his divorce was finalized, he'd made a vow to his son to be the best father he could. Like his own father had been before his death. Pete Mitchell was everything a man, husband and father should be.

Sierra yawned, rolling over so suddenly that Lizzie tipped forward. She woke with a start, throwing her hands out in front of her, sheer terror lining her face—until she opened her eyes. Even then, there was no hiding her struggle to shut down her fear.

Maybe, since she wasn't going anywhere, he'd get the chance to learn more about Lizzie Vega's ghosts and help her face them—if she wanted his help. What surprised him was how much he hoped she would.

Lizzie woke up with a start. She'd gone from blissfully warm and wrapped up to…not. And, now that she'd taken a minute to reacquaint herself with her surroundings, she saw why. Sierra slept on her back, her legs sticking up in the air and her tongue flopping out the side of her mouth. *Talk about the epitome of relaxation.* If she'd had a camera, she'd have taken a picture.

But she didn't.

Her camera was back home, in Houston, three hours away—through the rain and hail and thunder and lightning. She risked a look out the windows lining the back wall of the Mitchell family's home and frowned.

It was still raining.

Granted, the hail had stopped and, from what she could see and hear, so had the thunder and lightning but… The rain hadn't let up. She swallowed her sigh and slowly, carefully, pushed herself off the thick throw rug she and Sierra had dozed off on. Sierra, of course, instantly woke up—rising on all four paws to wag her tail.

"I didn't mean to wake you up," she said, stooping to give her a scratch behind the ear.

"Pretty sure she doesn't mind," Hayden said, peering around the corner of his laptop.

"I'm so sorry." She stretched her arms out behind her and slowly rolled her head. "You're seeing me at my worst, I fear. First my earlier behavior and now falling asleep on your floor. Honestly, though, I'm not sure how…" She nodded at the rain. Sleep was yet another thing affected by the storm. When she managed to get some, she treasured it.

His light brown eyes swept over her. "Are you warm enough?"

She nodded, glancing down at her sandal-covered feet, one of her favorite flowing layered skirts and heavy-stitched tunics. She'd set out under blue skies and soaring heat—her outfit had been completely appropriate. Now, not so much. That was the thing about Texas weather. A person could experience every season in one day—there was just no telling.

"Looks like you're here for at least tonight. The news said the Waldrip Bridge washed out. That's the other way out—behind us." He tilted his head, indicating the general direction. "Which means, until the water is down, you're stuck."

She nodded. "Should I be worried about my car?" She smiled as Sierra flopped down on the floor next to Charley.

"No. I called Walt, the owner of the gas station and a buddy of mine. He'll keep an eye on things." He picked a green apple from a bowl on the kitchen counter and took a big bite.

"It won't...wash away or anything?" She perched on one of the stools next to the marble-topped bar that separated the kitchen from the rest of the great room.

"Nah. Walt's place is on a higher elevation." He wiped his mouth with the back of his forearm. "Times like this are good for business. Folks get stranded and tend to hang around in his little café until things blow over."

Lizzie was beyond thankful that she'd wound up here versus stranded at Walt's diner on the side of the highway. Something told her she'd be far less calm there. "Well, thank you. Again." She paused. "And, if you have things to do, please don't feel like you have to entertain me. Honestly, I'd rather do something…" It helped reduce the likelihood of her having another panic attack. A little.

"What did you have in mind?" He finished off his apple.

"Apple pie? I can bake, if you like?" she asked, eyeing the bowl of apples. "I'll clean up whatever mess I make. If you like apple pie, that is."

His light brown gaze narrowed. "I didn't realize that was a real question."

She laughed. "I'll take that as a yes." She slid off the stool. "Just sort of point me in the right direction?" He did. While she was collecting the measuring cups and spoons, and butter and eggs from the refrigerator, he collected a number of items from the pantry. "Thank you."

"I'm the one who should be thanking you." He set the flour and sugar on the countertop.

"Maybe you should taste it first?" she teased, glancing his way. When his eyes met hers, she was instantly caught by the warmth in his gaze. His charming crooked half grin changed, turning into an honest-to-goodness smile. And what a smile. It was sort of mesmerizing…so much so that she almost dropped the cinnamon she'd originally planned to put with the rest of the ingredients. Breathe. *In. Out.* Sort of like her calming exercises…but without the panic. She was all warm and tingly instead. Because, really, how could she not be completely distracted by the smile and the height and breadth and overall gorgeousness of Hayden Mitchell?

Interestingly enough, he seemed a bit distracted himself. His tawny gaze swept over her face in a leisurely fashion—as if he were taking internal notes. Which could be good. Or bad. After today… She swallowed. *Very bad.* After all, how could a man who had seen her emotional pendulum swing from one extreme to another—over the course of hours—form a flattering opinion of her?

And it's not like it mattered. She'd be a blip in his life. A random, slightly unhinged woman he'd offered shelter to. It was different for her. Chances were this trip, and this man, would be etched on her memory for a long time to come. Partly because he'd offered her shelter when she really needed it. And partly because nothing and nobody had been able to make her forget, even for a second, what she'd been struggling with since she'd come out of that pantry a little over four months ago.

Yet, he had. And so had Sierra.

She was only just becoming aware of the distant

flash of lightning outside. And the building roar of thunder.

Hayden seemed just as surprised as she was. When his gaze shifted from her to the window, a deep V formed between his brows. "Guess it was too much to hope for the storm to be moving on."

She shrugged, willing her fight-or-flight instincts to behave. *Get a grip.*

A sudden increase in the storm's volume had her glancing at the back door. Charley stood, using his paw and nose to pull down the handle and tugging the door open.

"What is he doing?" she asked, an apple in her hand. "I thought you were joking."

"I wish I was." Hayden nodded at Charley. "Guess you need to go out?"

She watched as the dog trotted onto the back porch, ears and tail at attention, as he stared into the darkening sky. "Is it safe?"

"He's just checking things out." Hayden nodded. "Won't take long before he changes his mind and heads right back in."

Sure enough, five minutes later, Charley had returned to his sleeping spot—the back door closed behind him.

Charley had closed the door, too? He'd opened it. Why wouldn't he close it?

She laughed at the I-told-you-so look on Hayden's face and went back to pie making. The entire time she was coring and peeling apples, she was repeating Grammy's recipe in her head. As she was layering pats of butter, sugar and cinnamon, apples and more, she was silently doing multiplication tables. Once the pie was in the oven, the timer was set and she was washing dishes, she'd moved on to humming.

"Beatles fan?" Hayden said, glancing her way from the desk on the far side of the living room.

"What?" she asked, using a sponge to wipe down the counters.

"You're humming. Isn't that 'Hey Jude'?"

"Oh, yes." She smiled, spraying the counter with cleaning fluid. "I love the Beatles. My grammy had an extensive collection of vinyl records I remember listening to over and over when I'd visit. Once she decided to sell her home, she gave them all to me." She shrugged. "I had to go buy a record player but it was worth it."

"Pretty sure the counters have never been this clean." He sat back in his chair.

"Right." She rinsed out the sponge and stepped back, searching for something to help blot out the howl of the wind outside. "Well…"

The sudden whimper-cry from the baby monitor on Hayden's desk made her jump. "Naptime's over." Hayden smiled, checking his watch. "That boy is like clockwork." He stood. "This time I will show you where you'll be sleeping, if you like."

"Yes." This time she didn't have a lap full of Sierra to calm her down. "Sounds great." Not that she'd sleep. It didn't matter how comfy the bed or how soft the sheets were, she wouldn't get any sleep with it storming outside.

She trailed after him into Weston's room, all the more enchanted by the sweetness between Hayden and his son.

"Da da da," Weston cooed, smiling broadly, as Hayden lifted him from his crib.

"Good dreams?" Hayden asked, carrying him to the diaper table and changing his son without batting an eye. "You're smiling, so I guess so."

Weston kicked and squirmed and made delighted baby sounds, growing impatient when his father tried to get him back into his pants. Not that Hayden noticed. The man seemed unflappable. Then again, he'd been a soldier. He'd probably been in far more severe circumstances than a toddler's diaper change—no matter how fidgety Weston was.

Hayden scooped up Weston. "Better?"

Weston smiled, pressing both hands against Hayden's chest.

"Want to walk?" Hayden asked, squatting and putting Weston's feet on the ground. "He's pretty steady but sometimes, when he gets excited, his legs can't quite keep up."

For the first time, Weston noticed her in the doorway. He waved at her, his little fingers opening and closing.

"Hi, Weston." She waved back. "You're going to walk?"

Weston turned into Hayden's chest, peeking at her once, then again, and giggling.

"Are you playing peekaboo with me?" she asked, kneeling on the floor and covering her face, then peeking around them.

He giggled again. "Boo!"

"I thought so." She covered her face, then popped out again. "Peekaboo, I see you." She covered her face again, but when she moved her hands this time he was standing in front of her—clapping his hands and giggling.

"I'm glad you had a good nap, Weston." She tapped the tip of his nose. "I'm not sure your daddy has told you, but you have the sweetest smile."

As if on cue, Weston smiled at his father. "Da da."

"That's me. And he's my little speed walker." Hayden nodded. "Aren't you, Weston? Go? You want to go?"

Weston squealed, bouncing his little legs and clapping his hands. But he was clapping his hands so hard he threw off his balance. And, once he was sitting on his rear, little Weston didn't look so happy. Nope. His smile was gone and the little guy flipped his lower lip, so pathetic and precious Lizzie couldn't help herself.

"Oh, no." Lizzie held out her hands, gently helping him back to his feet. "That sad face is too...too..."

"I know." Hayden shook his head. "Gets me every time."

Lizzie wasn't sure which was sweeter: Weston's smile when he reached up for her or Hayden's devotion to his son. Or that, the entire time they'd been in Weston's nursery, she'd totally forgotten about the storm.

Chapter Seven

The storm died down to a steady sprinkle by late afternoon. On the outside, Lizzie seemed to be less troubled. But no matter how he'd tried to help cook and clean, she insisted that he needed to "let her do something." Once he understood what she needed, he got out of the way. For the most part.

He and Weston played with his toys—then asked if she wanted help. He and Weston read some books—then asked if she needed help. He and Weston played peekaboo and threw the ball for Charley and Sierra. But when he paused long enough to look her way, she said, "No, thank you, Hayden. I've got this."

After that, he made a blanket fort. For the next

hour, Weston contentedly dragged all of his toys and books and both dogs inside the small shelter.

"They're half in." Lizzie laughed. "And both their tails are wagging."

From the look on his son's face, Hayden wasn't the only one partial to the sound of Lizzie's laugh. Even more so when Weston started giggling in response.

Dinner was a perfectly cooked pot roast, soft-as-butter potatoes and carrots with a light sweet glaze that Weston couldn't get enough of. Hayden sat at the dinner table, eyeing the food—plus the basket of fresh-baked biscuits—and shook his head. "Lizzie, this is above and beyond."

She shook her head. "Not in my grammy's house it's not. This was a staple Sunday dinner at my mother's table, too. Considering the extreme kindness you and your family have shown me, decent food seems like the least I can do." She shrugged. "Besides, it's all your food—I just...cooked it."

"Cooked it?" He shot her a look. Yes, she'd cooked and cleaned and set the table with good china, little plates with pats of butter and a full gravy boat. "It looks more like Thanksgiving or Christmas."

"Or a nice thank-you meal." Her eyebrows rose as she spoke, her hands on her hips for added emphasis.

Weston sat, strapped into his high chair, watching the back-and-forth while chowing down on the carrots she'd sliced and put onto his tray. He jabbered, mimicking their tone and conversation with all sorts of facial expressions. Like, whatever he was saying, it was of the utmost importance. It was one of those things his son did that always made Hayden smile.

"You don't say," Lizzie answered Weston. "More carrots?" She placed a baby carrot on his tray.

Weston slapped his tray and smiled. He held up the carrot in his fingers and looked at Lizzie. "Ca?"

"Carrot." She nodded.

"Is that what he said?" Hayden asked, his smile growing. "I didn't know you were also fluent in toddler."

She and Weston both regarded him with wide eyes.

"Sorry." He held his hands up. "Didn't mean to interrupt." He watched as Lizzie cut up more carrots and one small potato and placed the food on Weston's tray.

Weston nodded, looked up at Lizzie and made a singsong noise. "Num nums."

"Thank you for saying thank you." Lizzie smiled. "And you're welcome. Eat up, yum."

Hayden watched his son do just that.

"You too, Hayden." She sat at the table across from him. "It won't taste nearly as good once it's cold." She paused. "I made your mother some broth, too. Just in case."

"You didn't have—"

"I wanted to." Her hazel eyes met his.

One look was as potent as a live wire—he felt it

in his bones. As much as he didn't want to overanalyze *why* a woman he'd known for maybe eight hours
was causing such an unfamiliar reaction, there was
no denying he was reacting. The hair on the back of
his neck pricked up. The warm pressure rising into
his chest. The odd tightness in his lungs and throat.

And, dammit, the urge to touch her. That was the
most troublesome of them all.

"What do you think?" Lizzie asked, pointing at
his plate with her fork. "Have you taken a bite?"

Weston, who had now managed to mash several
pieces of carrot into the wisp of his light brown hair,
watched, tucking the first two fingers of his right
hand into his mouth.

He obligingly scooped up a fork full and tried it.
"It's delicious, Lizzie. Best meal I've had in a long
time—but I'll deny that to my mother."

"As any good son should." She smiled.

"You like cooking?" he asked.

"Sure." She shrugged. "When there's nothing else
to do."

"Nothing else as in?" He kept eating, enjoying
every bite.

She skewered a small potato. "Art. I tend to sketch
or paint or sculpt… It's a great way to preoccupy
the brain."

He nodded. Preoccupation was a big thing for
her. "But you enjoy it, too? Don't you? It's not just a
means to keep your mind off…things."

"Oh, no. I love it." She nodded. "There's nothing as rewarding as creating. My brain sort of comes up with images or concepts, pretty much nonstop. Not that it ever turns out exactly as I imagined it, of course. But I do try." A little shrug. "Cooking is the same, when you think about it. Creating something—but something that's edible. A pretty table only makes it that much more art-like, I suppose."

It wasn't hard to imagine her creating something. Watching her in the kitchen had been revealing. Whether she was tasting or stirring or pulling things from a cabinet—she was lost in her own world. He'd assumed she was focused on her cooking, but now he asked, "Is that what you were thinking about today? A few times I caught you staring off, thinking about something. I'm assuming it wasn't the potatoes—though they are the best damn potatoes I've ever tasted."

She smiled, shaking her head. The slight movement was enough to jingle her earrings and catch Weston's eye. Weston was clearly pretty enamored with Lizzie. "No. I was thinking about that tree." With her fork, she pointed over her shoulder. "It needs a tree house."

"Does a tree house count as art?" he asked, finishing the food on his plate and leaning back in his chair.

"The one I dreamed up does." Her brows rose high. "What about you, Hayden? What does a rancher who's also a soldier and dog-human match-maker do in his spare time?"

"I'm not sure I'm all that?" Hayden asked, carrying his plate to the sink and rinsing it off. "You're looking at it." He winked at his son.

Weston gave him a huge smile. "Da da da da da."

"I can't think of a better way to spend time." She leaned forward, tapping Weston's little nose.

"You want kids?" Where the hell had that come from? That was none of his damn business. "Sorry."

"I do, one day. Yes." She didn't seem the least offended by his question. "I was engaged, several years ago. Brian, that was his name, had a little girl from his first marriage. Fiona." Lizzie's smile dimmed. "She was probably the reason the engagement lasted as long as it did, really. When we called it off, losing her was much harder than losing him."

Her honesty was refreshing. He hesitated but, in the end, curiosity won out. "What happened?"

"With my engagement?" A flash of panic crossed her face. "Or…"

"Your engagement." He knew better than to bring up the rest.

"I wasn't ready to have children. Not yet—not then. My mother worked hard, her whole life. She'd wanted me to get a degree, a career, to be someone. I owed it to her to do that." She stood, her empty plate in hand. "He said he understood. Besides, he had Fiona and said he was fine waiting."

"Let me." He reached across the table and took her plate, rinsing it off and adding it to the dishwasher.

"The thing is, he lied. He didn't want to wait. We broke up and he got married a couple of months later. Last I heard, he was expecting his second child with his new wife. His new wife knows one of my cousins—so I get to hear about it. Fun for me, right?" She sighed, glancing his way. "I guess I wasn't worth waiting for."

His loss. Thankfully, he didn't say *that* out loud. But he did say, "My ex decided she didn't want kids after he was here."

Lizzie stared at him, in shock. "She…" She swallowed hard, blinking rapidly. "How could…"

"I guess parenthood isn't for everyone." After the few counseling sessions and countless arguments they'd had, Hayden had finally come to terms with that.

"I'm sorry, Hayden." She was up, crossing the room, to stand a few inches from him.

"Weston and I get on just fine." He smiled down at her, surprised by the true sympathy in her large eyes. "Mom likes having us around, I think. She says Weston helps keep her young." He found himself waiting to see what she'd say or do next.

This close, the urge to touch her was stronger than ever.

Her hands sort of fluttered by her sides before she drew in a deep breath. "Well, I think pie is in order."

"No argument here." She liked to talk with her hands, he'd noticed.

She reached out and squeezed his arm. "Pie it is." With another strange hand flutter, she busied herself with the pie.

Five minutes later, she was offering him a plate piled high with pie and ice cream. "The crust didn't turn out as light as I'd hoped, but I think it's still edible."

He took a bite and moaned. "Your idea of edible and my idea of edible are entirely different things."

Weston watched with excited eyes. "Num num."

"You said it." Hayden scooped a small bite of cinnamon-sugar-coated apples on his spoon and offered it to Weston. His grabbed the spoon and made short work of the treat. "I think he's a fan, too. Pie, Weston. It's yum yum pie."

Other than Weston's delight over dessert, they enjoyed their pie in companionable silence. This wasn't normal, not for him, anyway. It took time for him to accept a person, to feel at ease in their presence. Here he sat, laughing and having pie, with a woman he barely knew.

Barely knew but who still triggered a response unlike anything he'd ever felt.

While she put away the pie and straightened up the kitchen, he gave Weston a bath—doing his best to make his son's hair carrot free. Lucky for him, Weston was a fan of bath time so the extra scrubbing didn't faze his son in the least. Once he was squeaky clean, Hayden bundled him up and carried him to his nursery.

"You ready for bed?" he asked, smiling down at his son.

Weston grabbed his toes and giggled.

"I'm thinking that's a no." He shook his head. "Maybe I need Lizzie in here to translate."

Weston clapped his hands and giggled again—but this time he yawned and rubbed his eyes. Hayden was leaving the nursery as Lizzie was headed into the guest room. He'd already shown her where the extra linens were located and rounded up some unopened travel-sized toiletries his mother collected whenever she stayed overnight for one of her scrapbooking shows.

"Night," she said, a little too pale and wide-eyed for his liking. But Sierra was at her side.

Good sign. "Have everything you need?"

"Nope. I mean yes." The shaking of her head was fast—agitated. "I'm good."

He sighed. "If you need anything, I'm straight that way." He pointed. "All the way at the end."

She nodded, her gaze darting from him to her bedroom door to Sierra and back again. "Okay." She stepped inside and closed the door behind Sierra.

It took him a while to fall asleep—and he didn't stay that way for long. A little after three in the morning, his eyes popped open. He lay there, half-asleep and disoriented, when he realized what was wrong.

The power was out. Weston's baby monitor.

He stood, tugged on his jeans and headed across the great room to the bedrooms on the other side of the house—pausing long enough to grab the flashlight under the kitchen sink. Charley, who'd been sleeping on his mat by the back door, trailed after him. If Weston was crying, he couldn't tell. The storm was raging outside, so loud that he couldn't hear much else. Normally, Weston slept through pretty much anything. But today had been anything but normal.

Not that he had any complaints. Not at all. Panic aside, he enjoyed spending time with Dr. Elizabeth Vega.

However, he hadn't expected to find her in Weston's nursery. She sat in the rocking chair—wrapped up in a quilt with Weston in her arms, rocking. Sierra was sprawling on the floor between the chair and the bed. If the chair hadn't been rocking so steadily, he might have believed they were all asleep. But he knew better.

Weston had likely woken up, crying, and Lizzie had made her way here to comfort his son—even though she was likely the one in need of comfort.

She kept on counting… It would be so much easier if the thunder wasn't shaking the house. Or lightning wasn't causing the window in Weston's room to flash with each strike. And the wind… Not as bad as a hurricane wind—there was nothing like that. She was doing well. No panic attack, not yet. But it was enough to have her on high alert.

Eyes glued shut, rocking and counting.

Weston's weight in her arms.

Sierra sprawled atop one foot.

If she kept focusing on that… Well, she'd just keep focusing.

"Lizzie?" A whisper. A touch.

Her eyes fluttered open. "Hayden?" He'd pointed his flashlight toward the floor, casting just enough light to see him.

"You okay?" Hayden's voice was pitched low.

"He was crying," Lizzie whispered. He'd been crying and crying and she'd had no choice but to check on him. "The power went out… I used my flashlight as a night-light." And once Weston had fallen into a sweet sleep, the feel of him in her arms and Sierra draped across her feet had been so calming she'd stayed put. Storm aside, she'd been all too content to sit and rock awhile.

He stared down at her. "Thank you."

She nodded, smiling down at the sound-asleep Weston. "My pleasure." And it had been, too—for the most part.

He held his hand out to her. "Let me help you get him back into bed."

She took the hand, ignoring the instant tingle and heat his touch sparked, and let him pull her from the comfy rocking chair. Sierra moved too, taking her anchoring weight and warmth with her. *It's fine.* The window rattled from the storm. *Everything is fine.* It was with great reluctance that she placed Weston back in his crib.

Together, they tiptoed from his room. The four of them, Hayden, Lizzie and the two dogs, stood outside Weston's nursery, the beam of the flashlight the only light. No lights. No power. No baby monitor. She didn't feel right, leaving Weston alone. "How will you hear him?"

"I'll go find some batteries." He ran a hand over his head and stifled a yawn. "And I'll get the generator running."

"I'll feel better waiting here—until the batteries are located, if that's okay?" Did that sound weird? *Like he doesn't already know I'm weird.*

"I'd appreciate that." He pressed the flashlight into her hand. "Here."

"You won't need one?" It was dark. *Dark* dark. "To find batteries? Where is the generator?"

"No worries." He was already walking away. "They're both in the shop, where we parked. I know my way around."

The shop? "You mean the place full of saws and tools and horror-movie-worthy farm implements? You're going there, in the dark?" Add in the storm and this whole thing had the makings of a perfect horror movie.

"I have to say, I've never thought about it that way. Horror movie, huh?" His chuckle was warm and…lovely. "Pretty sure I could navigate the place blindfolded."

"Which is basically what you're doing," she pointed out. Without the flashlight, it would be pitch-black.

"I'll be back." His hand offered hers a quick squeeze before he headed down the hall.

She stood, waiting, but her calming breaths weren't doing a thing to keep her calm. The next clap of thunder almost had her dropping the flashlight.

Sierra pressed her nose against her hand, that low doggie moan-whimper noise rumbling from the back of her throat.

"Are you telling me to chill?" she asked.

Sierra's tail picked up.

"If I could, I would. Believe me." Instead, she paced the hallway, Sierra pacing at her side.

It was taking too long. Way too long. What if… No, those two words opened the door to her overactive imagination. And, since the hurricane, her overactive imagination tended to go down a dark path. Like picturing Hayden being trapped in the shop or pinned underneath something or having some lethal tool or piece of equipment—knocked loose by the wind—hurling at him. Imagining him hurt... *Way to picture the* absolute *worst-case scenario.*

She hadn't realized she was heading to the great room, through the kitchen and to the door into the shop until the light over the stove flickered on and the digital clocks started blinking. The power was back on. She clicked off the flashlight—and slammed into Hayden's chest. His big, broad, warm and very solid chest.

His hands caught her shoulders, steadying her. "You good?"

She nodded, staring at his chest. His bare chest. She sucked in long, deep breaths to steady her thundering heart. Clearly, he was fine. And she'd overreacted. And now that the lights were on and she was face-to-face with his very muscular, very broad, very *naked* chest, she accepted that the likelihood of her heart rate returning to normal anytime soon was almost zero.

"You sure?" His voice dropped low.

"I tend to have a very vivid imagination." She cleared her throat. "Considering the various doomsday scenarios in the shop, I..."

His hands rubbed up and down her upper arms, sending the most distracting tingles up her arms and down her spine. "Doomsday scenarios, huh?" The words were edged with amusement.

"Like I said, vivid imagination." Her imagination was moving in a very different direction now. His hands were so warm. And his chest was... Well, it was *right* there. *He* was right there. She swallowed.

His voice deepened. "And you were coming to rescue me?"

She swallowed. Had that been the plan? What had she been thinking? "I hadn't gotten that far yet." She glanced up at him.

Between the light from the stove and the one on the back porch, it was bright enough to see him. Really see him. Looking at her with an intensity that made her insides soften. Which was ridiculous, wasn't it? Except it wasn't. The spark between them was palpable. A magnetic current drawing them together. It was happening. Right now.

His fingertips traced the curve of her jaw.

"This is the strangest day of my life," she whispered, entirely focused on him. His touch. His gaze. His proximity.

"Agreed." His voice was low, gruff and toe-curling.

"I'm not complaining." She wasn't breathing. Was she? Did it matter?

"Agreed." He stepped forward, his hand resting against her cheek. "But that's not going to stop me from asking if I can—"

"Kiss me," she finished, sliding her hands up his chest, his impossibly warm, wall-like chest, and around his neck. "Yes, please."

It was the softest sweep of his lips against hers,

but potent enough to induce a full-body shudder from her and a ragged—bone-melting—hitch in his breath.

He lifted his head, just as caught off guard as she was...

But then her hands gripped his shoulders, his arm slid around her waist and she was pressed against him. Being wrapped up in Hayden Mitchell's arms was just as intense as he was. His lips met hers and every single fiber of her being was alive with want. Every sensation seemed magnified. The firmness of his mouth against hers. The cling of his lips, seeking... And when she opened for him, the sweep of his tongue against hers.

No breathing. No thinking. Just this. Just him.

Thankfully, he seemed to be on the same page. His hand sliding beneath her shirt, his warm palm pressed against the base of her spine. She was arching into him when his fingertips made a slow incline up, between her shoulders.

It took a minute to realize an overhead light had come on.

Another to disentangle herself from Hayden.

Thirty seconds more to realize who'd turned on the light...and accept that *this* was how she was meeting Hayden's mother.

"I...I..." The woman was staring back and forth between them, her eyes round as saucers. "Toast," she managed, then cleared her throat, dousing the light switch panel with a blast of antibacterial spray.

"I thought I'd make myself a piece of toast." Her gaze, darker than her son's, regarded her with open curiosity. "Thank you for the soup."

Say something. *Speak.* "You're welcome. I'm glad you're feeling a little better." Lizzie tried to make her sidestep away from Hayden casual. "I'm Lizzie. Lizzie Vega." Hayden was staring at the floor.

"Jan Mitchell Simmons." The woman smiled, holding the antibacterial spray to her chest. "I'd shake your hand, but I wouldn't wish this bug on my worst enemy. Not that I have one."

Lizzie smiled. "How about I make you some toast?" She nodded at the spray. "It's the least I can do, Mrs. Mitchell Simmons."

"Jan." She nodded. "I won't say no."

"Mom." Hayden ran a hand over his head. "I can bring it to you in your room, if you want."

"Oh, no." Jan shook her head, a small smile on her face. "I'll wait for my toast. Right here."

Lizzie caught the look between mother and son but didn't know what it meant. At the moment, she knew only one thing. She was mortified. And Hayden was still very shirtless. *Okay, two things.* Just thinking about what the woman had walked in on had her cheeks flaming. Standing there, blushing, wouldn't help a thing, so she headed to the pantry for the bread when Hayden cut her off.

"I've got it, Lizzie." Hayden reached around her

to grab the pantry doorknob. "You can go on to bed. I can take care of my mother. It's been a long day."

If it wasn't for the irritation in his voice, she'd have stayed. She didn't relish the idea of tossing and turning in a strange bed since the storm was still very much underway—even with Sierra at her side. But he *was* irritated. From the look on his face, very irritated. She had sort of thrown herself at him. Wait, he'd been asking if he could kiss her. Hadn't he? Those words hadn't actually come out of his mouth—since she'd been too busy pressing her mouth to his. *Oh, no.*

"Okay." She stepped aside, aware of the space he was keeping between them. "I *am* tired." And mortified that she'd been caught kissing Hayden. And far too preoccupied by his shirtlessness—in front of his mother, no less. "I hope the toast helps settle your stomach."

Jan nodded, watching them like a hawk. "Me, too."

"Night, then." She paused, glancing at Hayden.

"Good night, Lizzie." He didn't look at her. His tone, his posture—it was like nothing had happened. Nothing at all. Maybe it was normal for him to kiss someone he'd known for under twenty-four hours, but for her it was not.

With a nod, she headed toward her room. It was only when she'd flopped onto the bed, Sierra at her side, that she allowed herself to consider what might have happened if Jan hadn't come into the kitchen.

Chapter Eight

Hayden put the bread in the toaster and waited until the click-click of Sierra's nails faded, followed by the closing of a door, before facing his mother.

She was sitting on a kitchen stool, resting her chin in her hands. "Well?"

He shook his head. He had no idea what the hell had just happened. Only that he'd do it all again.

"Don't you shake your head at me." His mother frowned. "She is lovely."

She is. Beautiful. Soft. Passionate. And yet, he barely knew her.

"And she's here for work?" she asked.

"Sort of." The toast popped so he put it on a paper

towel and slid it across the counter to his mother. "She needs a companion animal. Sierra seems to have figured that out." The dog was oddly in tune with Lizzie—like they'd known each other for a long time. *I know the feeling.* He shook his head. "Never seen anything like it." Which was true. He wanted Sierra to have a solid bond with her owner. He wanted the dog to take care of Lizzie. And he wanted Lizzie to... Well, he wanted *her*.

"What happened to her?" She nibbled on the corner. "Is she all right?"

"I don't know the details, but she's been through something. Something to do with the hurricane. She has a real phobia of storms." Which was putting it mildly. He went to retrieve a clean undershirt from the dryer before heading back into the kitchen. He leaned against the kitchen counter, thinking through the information Mark had shared and the information she'd mentioned. It wasn't hard to put some of the dots together. Houston was still recovering from one of the most devastating hurricanes in the last twenty years. He'd seen the devastation and cleanup of the aftermath. Lizzie had been there for that—something had happened to her...

"And you like her," his mother said.

Yes. The answer was there, without hesitation. The fact that he knew so little about her didn't affect the answer. He liked her. But he wasn't fool enough to say as much to his mother. His mother was a total romantic. "Mom—"

"It was a statement, not a question, Hayden James." She shook her head. "What I just walked in on... Well, I have to admit I've been worried about you. You don't exactly have an *active* social life."

"We are not having this conversation." He shook his head.

"Fine. We won't." She shrugged and took another bite of toast. "But I'm guessing she will be stuck out here for the next two days or so, since the roads are washed out."

He nodded. It had been a while since he'd been stranded in one place. Normally, it made him itch to get out. But he'd already accepted that there was nothing normal about anything that had happened in the last day. Was that it? Less than a day? And, somehow, he had developed a connection to this woman? A *real* connection? No, that wasn't possible. He was attracted to her, clearly... What the hell had he been thinking? Touching her? Holding her? Kissing her? He swallowed, the feel of her lips against his lingering.

He'd let things get way too out of control. He never let things get out of control.

"Good." His mother slipped off her stool and picked up her toast. "It gives me a little time to get to know her."

He shook his head. "She's going back to Houston

as soon as the roads clear." Was he telling his mother that? Or reminding himself? Right now, they were caught up in a singularly unusual situation. But it wouldn't last forever. The rain would stop and they'd both go back to their regular lives. A quick glance out the window showed him the rain was still coming down.

"I guess we'll see. Thank you for the toast. I'm heading to bed." She waved and sprayed down the stool she'd been sitting on. "Weston will be up in a couple of hours."

"You rest tomorrow, Mom." He saw the relief on her face and smiled. "I've got Weston covered."

"Thank you. I think I'll need it." She blew him a kiss and went to her room.

Charley sat, tail thumping, lifting one paw. Hayden knew what that meant.

"Now you're hungry?" he asked.

Charley's tail kept on thumping.

Hayden gave Charley a teeth-cleaning chew treat and stared down the hall—where his mother and Weston and Lizzie were sleeping. It was quiet. Very quiet.

Lizzie. Was she sleeping? Could she, with the rain still beating against the roof?

Or was she still trying to wrap her head around what had just happened between them? Because he sure as hell was. For a handful of minutes, he'd been so caught up in her the rest of the world had ceased to exist. That didn't happen. Not for him. Not *ever*.

Until today.

And yet, in the back of his mind, he could hear Karla throwing his "hero complex" in his face. She said his need to be needed, to fix things—be the knight in shining armor—then distancing himself once the problem was taken care of was selfish. He didn't do good to help others. He did it to make himself feel good.

Until now, he'd believed Karla had been looking for a guilt-free excuse to end their marriage. But… Could there be some truth to what she'd said?

Karla had been recovering from her first divorce when they'd started dating. And yes, he'd always dropped everything when his mother or his brothers or his unit needed him. Was that wrong? Was it bad that he enjoyed being needed—enjoyed *doing* for others?

But the other? Had he put distance between them when Karla had been strong enough to stand on her own two feet? When her career was taking off? Had he been as supportive as he could have been? He thought he had. Maybe he *was* the selfish ass she accused him of being.

His little brother John would probably agree. After Ed's true colors came out, John had accused Hayden of being too busy trying to fill the role of their father to be the brother and friend he needed.

The more he thought about it, the heavier his chest felt.

He needed to do better—for his son, his mother and his brothers. They were his family, what mattered most in his world, no matter what. After all he'd seen and done in his life, he realized just how important they were to him. It was up to him to make sure they knew that.

And Lizzie? He blew out a long, slow breath. It was two, three days tops and she'd be gone. A blip in time. Certainly not enough time to develop legitimate feelings for someone. Sure, the attraction was real enough, but she was wounded—vulnerable. He didn't want to add to that.

He shook his head, pinching the bridge of his nose. *Enough.* He wasn't going to spend any more time thinking about or worrying over this—over *nothing.* They'd kissed. Once. It wouldn't happen again. That was a promise.

"Come on, Charley." He flipped off the kitchen light and spent the next three hours tossing and turning and getting next to no sleep. Every crash of thunder reminded him of Lizzie's haunted gaze. Every time he dozed off, she was back in his arms—his lips hungry on hers. *Dammit.* The harder he tried not to think of her, the more he thought of her. At six he gave up, kicked off the covers and took a fast shower. He made a pot of coffee, fed Charley and stared out the back window.

Blue skies for miles. *Better.* With any luck, the sun would stay out long enough to start drying things out. The sooner things got back to normal, the better. And, by *normal*, he meant Lizzie Vega—safe and sound—back in her world where she belonged. Far enough away that his overwhelming preoccupation with her would fade.

Coffee in hand, he crept as quietly as possible down the hall to Weston's room. His boy had had a rough night, and chances were he was still sleeping. Or not.

"You like that one best?" Lizzie. She was smiling, he heard it in her voice.

"Ba." Weston. "Ba."

"I like this ball, too. It's blue." She laughed. "No, Sierra. It's Weston's ball."

Hayden ran a hand along the back of his neck. He hadn't had enough coffee for this. Last night was a fluke. *It wouldn't happen again.* That was the plan, anyway. He stared at the door. *Stick to the plan.*

He peered into the room to find Weston, dressed and smiling, rolling a ball to Lizzie. Rather, trying to. Sierra was sitting up, ears alert, watching the ball with her big brown eyes. And Lizzie… He barely noticed the wrinkled clothes and lopsided bun. She was smiling. It was the first genuine smile he'd seen since meeting her—and it knocked the air from his lungs. He'd thought she was beautiful before…

Two days. After that, she was gone. He had to remember that. He cleared his throat. "Good morning."

His son's smile was a ray of sunshine that never failed to warm his heart. "Da da." Weston managed to pull himself up on his crib and then barreled across the room, arms outstretched and with a wide, openmouthed grin.

He scooped Weston up and gave him a kiss on the cheek. "How's my boy?"

"Da da," Weston said, followed by a string of excited gibberish.

"You don't say? Tell me all about it." He nodded, barely glancing at Lizzie. "Morning."

"Good morning." She busied herself, returning the toys to Weston's toy chest.

He kept bouncing Weston, trying not to look at her. "Did he wake you up?"

"No." She stood, smoothing her skirts. "I was awake." She reached up, fiddling with her hair, smoothing the loose curls with her fingers. "Is it possible to take a shower?"

"A short one." He nodded. "I can find you something to wear, if you like."

"If it's no trouble." Her hazel eyes met his—and held.

He shook his head, unable to look away or stop the flood of sensation that rolled over him. Her touch. Her scent. Her kiss. He swallowed, hard, against the sudden tightness in his throat.

"Yum," Weston said, patting Hayden's chest. "Yum yum."

It was enough to sever the connection. She turned to Sierra and he sucked in a deep breath to say, "I'm hungry too, Weston." He bounced his son. "Let's get Lizzie taken care of and see what we can wrangle up for breakfast."

"I can wait." She made a silly face at Weston. "Yum yums come first. Always."

Weston giggled, clapping his hands.

"He agrees." Lizzie nodded, glancing his way to ask, "Can I make breakfast?"

"You took care of everything last night." He carried Weston out of the nursery and toward the kitchen. Besides, the busier he stayed, the less pre-occupied he'd be. Or at least he damn well hoped so. "I think I can handle some cereal and bananas and applesauce. If that's okay?" he asked, glancing over his shoulder at her.

To find her checking out his butt. And damn it all, if she kept looking at him like that, keeping his distance was going to be one hell of a challenge.

Lizzie wrapped a towel around her hair and slipped on the drawstring athletic pants Hayden's mother had loaned her. He'd also managed to find an unused toothbrush and travel toothpaste, and a comb. His mother was a good four inches taller than she was so she had to roll up the pants leg. But the

Army Mom shirt wasn't too big—and both of them were clean. After sleeping in her clothes, it was a nice change.

Not that she'd done much sleeping—as was evidenced by the dark smudges under her eyes.

It wasn't just the storm that kept her awake. It was Hayden… More specifically, what she and Hayden had done in the kitchen. Her love life had, until last night, been rather tame. Boring almost. A sad statement, considering she'd been engaged. But last night… Well, she'd never been swept away like that. Never been blindsided by something so intense and desperate. And she hadn't wanted it to stop—hadn't wanted him to let go. If his mother hadn't walked in, what would have happened?

Now, Hayden was putting Weston down for a nap, Jan had yet to make an appearance, and she and Hayden would be alone again. But, from his relatively cool demeanor, she suspected there wasn't much chance of a repeat performance. She didn't know how to feel about that. About any of this.

"Need anything else?" Hayden asked, from the other side of the bathroom door.

She opened the door, drying her hair with the towel before hanging it over the curtain rod. "No. Thank you. I feel tremendously better." A hot, if fast, shower. A beautiful sunshine-filled day. An adorable baby and the sweetest dog she'd ever met. And…Hayden.

Hayden—whose light brown eyes swept over her face and lingered on her mouth a little too long. "Good." He cleared his throat, stared at the floor and repeated, "Good." He turned on his heel and headed down the hall.

What was that?

She finished tidying the bathroom, grabbed her comb and headed into the great room.

Sunlight spilled in through the French doors, casting a large patch on the Spanish tile floor. Charley and Sierra lay, sprawled and snoring, in the swath of sunlight. It was a sweet picture, pure contentment.

Considering how sleep-deprived she was, the whole newness of her surroundings and being stranded, she was feeling surprisingly good. Even better if she managed to locate some sort of self-restraint when it came to Hayden Mitchell.

Like his butt. She was staring at it now… But his butt, in tight jeans, was worth admiring.

"Any news on the roads?" she asked, perching on the edge of the overstuffed leather sofa. She started combing through her thick, wet hair, her gaze bouncing his way before focusing on the brilliant blue skies outside.

"Still closed, I'm afraid." He sat in the leather armchair opposite her, his long legs stretched out in front of him. "You sure you don't need to let anyone know where you are?"

She worked the comb through her long dark

hair, picking out the knots with care. "If I called my grammy, she'd only worry. Me, alone, stranded with a stranger." She shook her head imagining her grandmother's reaction. "That would not do. She'd call the National Guard, the police, send out a search and rescue party."

"All that?" Hayden's forehead creased as he raised one eyebrow, the corner of his mouth kicking up.

"Probably best to let her think I'm home. Safe and sound." Lizzie was more than a little dazed by that crooked smile. "You don't mess with Grammy." She sounded breathless. *Pathetic.* With effort, she tore her gaze from his and shoved her comb back into her purse. "What about your mom? How is her stomach?"

"I peeked in on her while you were in the shower." He sat forward, resting his elbows on his knees. "Guess the toast and soup were a bad idea. She's greener today that she was yesterday."

"Oh, no." She tucked a strand of long, damp hair behind her ear and sat, legs crossed, on the couch. "Is there anything I can do?" Something. Anything. *The sooner the better.* Or she'd wind up staring at him. Since he'd walked into Weston's nursery, she'd been far too interested in *everything* about Hayden Mitchell.

He eyed Sierra and Charley, both sound asleep. "We could take them for a walk."

"Weston?" she asked.

"Monitor." He nodded at the baby monitor receiver. "Has close to a nine-hundred-foot radius—just in case."

"I...I don't want to take you away from work." She started braiding her hair. "You don't need to entertain me. I mean, you can, I don't know, pretend I'm not here."

He looked at her like she was growing another head, so incredulous that she had to laugh.

"What does that look mean?" she asked, still laughing, as she stretched the band out to hold her braid. "Do I want to know?" That crooked grin of his was back—sending a tremor the length of her spine and making her drop the hair band. She uncrossed her legs and bent to pick it up, chastising herself for overreacting. *Overreacting* wasn't the right word. It was more like she was hyperreactive—to him. He was watching her intently when she sat up. So intently that the band popped off her fingers and flew across the room. "Guess I won't braid it."

He didn't say anything. He didn't move. Well, other than the sudden clench of his jaw, that is.

The longer the silence stretched out, the thinner the air seemed to get. It would help if she knew what he was thinking versus inserting what she wanted him to be thinking. Things that involved less space between them, more touching—hands and lips... Her lungs emptied as she tore her gaze from his. She drew in a ragged breath. "I don't have shoes." She cleared her throat and glanced his way. "For walking. It's muddy."

He took a deep breath and stood. "There are some rubber gardening boots in the mudroom. Might be a little big for you, but it's better than ruining your sandals." He paused. "If you want to go on a walk, that is."

She nodded. "I'd like that." If she hadn't been in the middle of a panic attack when they arrived, she might have taken a better look at her surroundings. All she remembered was a lot of land and no other houses—and lots and lots of rain. Now, with the sun spilling in through the windows, she couldn't wait to see Hayden's family home. With any luck, some fresh air and sunshine might diffuse the tension between them.

He led her to the mudroom and shook out the boots, saying, "In case a scorpion climbed inside." Once he was satisfied, he held out the boots.

"Um." She peered inside; she couldn't help it. *Scorpion?* "You're sure?"

He grinned. "I'm sure." He waited, still holding the dark green pair of boots, looking devastatingly handsome and muscular and manly.

With a shake of her head, she took the boots and tugged them on. "Okay. I'm ready for rain puddles."

He grabbed the baby monitor, whistled and opened the side door leading into the shop. Charley and Sierra were up, trotting out the door, tails wagging.

"We have to go this way so we don't track mud in." He pressed the button, opening the large garage door, and glanced her way. "It's safe."

She gave the room a wary inspection. "It's not nearly as intimidating when the sun is shining. I guess that applies to most things, really."

He stopped just outside the open garage door, the sun beaming down on him. "You want to talk about it?" he asked, putting a well-worn straw cowboy hat on his head.

Oh, my. Hayden Mitchell, in a cowboy hat. She swallowed, focusing on putting one foot in front of the other and not the very pleasing picture he made. "Is this part of my dog-owner suitability screening? Or an attempt at conversation?" She glanced his way.

"Conversation." Tension bracketed his mouth.

"If it's all the same to you, I'd rather not ruin this beautiful day." She brushed past him and out of the garage. "Are you waiting on us?" she asked Sierra.

Sierra wagged her tail.

"She looks like she's smiling. Don't you think?" She glanced Hayden's way. Who knew she had a thing for cowboy hats? Then again, she'd never remembered having this sort of a reaction to a cowboy hat before. So…maybe it wasn't the hat so much.

He tilted his head to one side. "Guess so." He didn't look convinced.

"Are we headed somewhere in particular?" She followed Sierra across the yard to the wooden fence. But the sun, shining brightly in the cloudless blue sky, distracted her. If it wasn't for the squish of mud beneath her boot-clad feet, it was almost as if last night's torrential downpour never happened. She tilted her face back to soak up the warmth and light, eager to chase away any traces of the lingering anxiety the storm had left behind.

"Better?" he asked.

She shot him a look. "I'm assuming that's not a serious question." After all, he'd witnessed a few of her episodes up close and personal. She'd fallen apart and dragged him into it. "I am sorry." She cleared her throat. "For…" She pointed at herself, head to toe.

He frowned, resting his forearms on the top of the fence. "For?"

"My behavior." She winced. "I guess it's obvious I'm *struggling* with…something. But I sort of dumped *my* struggles onto *your* shoulders." Which were big and capable and broad. "I have no right to burden you just because I'm on edge and questioning *every* facet of my life. Do I want my job? Do I like my job? And my house… It's exhausting." *Stop talking.* Apologize and stop. "And now I just added that, didn't I? I'm sorry. Again. That wasn't fair. To do that. This." Another wince. "That's what for."

He was staring straight ahead, his expression neutral. "You don't owe me any apologies, Lizzie. I, on the other hand, owe you one."

"You do?" This was news to her. "As far as I'm concerned, you're sort of a real-life knight in shining armor. Helping the damsel in distress. That would be me—the damsel."

His frown was back, deeper than before. "I kissed you."

She stared at him, in shock. "You're apologizing for kissing me?" She'd been tossing in her bed, reliving that kiss—kisses—over and over. And he was sorry?

He looked at her then, his jaw clenched tight. "Yes."

"Oh." She paused, not wanting him to apologize for last night—the kissing—any of it. "If I remember things correctly, you did *ask* me first. I said yes. Then…I remember kissing you back."

"Still… It shouldn't have happened." His gaze pinned hers. "It won't happen again. You just said it, you're struggling with something. Sounds like you've got a lot to work through. It's been a while, but I don't remember a single knight in shining armor taking advantage of a damsel in distress." He sighed. "I wanted to check in on things at the barn. It's not too far."

She nodded, an awkward silence hanging between them.

One thing that became immediately apparent was the beauty of the land. The rain had left things bright and green and the air clean. In the distance, she saw a large barn with adjoining paddocks. Beyond that, endless fields with a herd of red-and-white cattle grazing. There was no denying the Mitchell ranch was impressive. Almost as impressive as the man walking at her side. A man who had just promised there would be no more kissing and apologized for what had been, for her, the best kiss of her life. She wasn't sure what troubled her more: that he regretted last night or that it wouldn't happen again.

Chapter Nine

Hayden rested his foot on the bar of the pipe fencing, watching the most recent addition to the ranch
snort and blow in the pen. This bull was important
to the ranch—he was a good start to getting their
finances back on track. *And one hell of a financial
investment.*

"He looks a little...aggressive." Lizzie was standing on the lower bar, resting her elbows on the top to
stare at the massive Hereford bull he'd been waiting
on. "Okay, a lot aggressive."

"He has the potential to be." Hayden nodded.
"He's good stock. Hardy. We're wanting to breed
him, bring in a new bloodline."

"Would he hurt the dogs?" Lizzie asked, glancing back and forth between the bull and Sierra and Charley. The dogs sat on a patch of grass between them, ears perked and eyes trained on the massive animal, assessing the bull. Her brow furrowed.

"He wouldn't take too kindly to the dogs venturing into his territory." Hayden replied. "But they're smart enough to know better."

Lizzie didn't look convinced. "Stay away from him, you hear me?" She spoke to the dogs, earning her excessive tail wagging from both of them. "He doesn't strike me as all that friendly."

Hayden shook his head, unable to stop himself from smiling. She was something, all right. Talking to the dogs like they understood. Then again, they were both looking at her like maybe they did. *No. They're dogs.* And he was sleep-deprived. "You ever ride?" he asked.

"What?" she asked, her hazel eyes shifting his way. "Horses?"

He paused, amused by her wide-eyed expression. "We have a barn full of them—if you're interested." The idea of her on a horse was oddly appealing. There were few things he enjoyed more than a long rambling ride across the property. It steadied his nerves, helped him clear his mind and focus on the things that really mattered. All things Lizzie would benefit from.

And knowing her, she'd probably talk to her horse,

too. He smiled at the thought—then frowned. What the hell was he thinking? This walk had been to get them out of the house, put space between them and ease the crackling attraction between them. That had been the plan. *It's not working.* Now he was contemplating putting her on horseback? *Very bad idea.* "Another time, maybe."

"Oh." Lizzie's brow furrowed a bit as she stepped down from the fence and tucked her wildly curly hair behind her ear.

Until now, Hayden hadn't noticed just how dark her hair was—almost blue-black. With the Texas sun beating, the long, silky strands were drying into glossy curls that seemed to dance in the warm, thick breeze. Like her skirts. Her bracelets. There was a movement to Lizzie... Spirit and beauty. *The walk was a bad idea. Dammit.* He stared down at the mud at his feet, his throat tight.

"Okay."

He ignored the disappointment in her voice. "I need to talk with our foreman, if you want to come. Damage check after last night." When she nodded, he followed the path to the barn doors.

He spied Bobby Doherty as soon as they entered the barn. His bright suspenders were impossible to miss. For all his no-nonsense practicality, his penchant for wild-patterned and colored suspenders was an oxymoron. Hayden knew the truth. Bobby adored his wife, Opal, who gifted him a new set of colorful or printed suspenders for every holiday or birthday.

After Ed had died, Hayden had fired his stepfather's foreman hire. Jerry Wilkes was one of Ed's old drinking buddies. He knew nothing about ranching, and his mismanagement of the place had only added to the financial strain Hayden was still unraveling. Bobby, who'd been doing the best he could as Jerry's right-hand man, had proved his worth. That was going on four years ago now. And every day since he'd hired Bobby, Hayden was thankful for the man's frugal sensibilities and deep loyalty.

"Hayden." Bobby shook his hand. "Been out this morning already. A few fences need new wire. I've got Clay out in the south field, checking the low spot. Hopefully, whatever debris has been caught won't have pulled the whole fence down."

Hayden nodded. The creek cut through the south pasture. When the water got high enough, like now, it filled up fast and drained into one of the tanks on the property—as long as there wasn't too much debris clogging it up. "Let me know."

Bobby's attention had strayed beyond him. "I didn't know we had a visitor on the place." His brows rose, his mouth pinched. One thing about Bobby, he wasn't keen on strangers underfoot. He had a suspicious nature. But, after working for Ed and with Jerry, Hayden couldn't exactly blame the man.

Hayden turned, spying Lizzie and the dogs in

front of one of the horse stalls. His heart picked up. *Dammit.* The urge to reach for her was just as strong, and misplaced, as ever. How could she look so damn beautiful wearing rolled-up athletic pants, an oversize T-shirt and mud-splattered rubber boots? Didn't matter. She was—so much so, it took effort to pull his gaze from her. Chief, his horse, had obligingly stuck his head over the stall door—his ears ticked forward to hear whatever Lizzie was saying. Of course, she was talking to the horse. He ran a hand over his head. "That's Dr. Elizabeth Vega." *Lizzie.* He turned back to Bobby. "Storm stranded her here."

"That's a shame." Some of the starch went out of his posture. "How did she get here in the first place?"

"I brought her out yesterday, after the roads washed out. She's adopting Sierra." As soon as he said it, he realized he'd made up his mind. The two of them had developed an instant, easy bond. He knew, with Sierra at her side, Lizzie would have the support she needed to get back on her feet. That's what he wanted—to know Lizzie would be okay. He swallowed hard.

"Well, that's good, then." Bobby nodded, giving Lizzie another once-over before turning his attention back to the clipboard he'd been making notes on. Bobby was old-school that way.

Hayden spent the next few minutes focusing on work and prioritizing damage control. They didn't get rains like this very often, so without doing a thorough once-over of the place, there was no way to know the full extent of the repairs needed. He and Bobby were so caught up in their growing to-do list he didn't realize Lizzie had joined them.

"Ma'am," Bobby said, taking off his hat, looking acutely uncomfortable.

"Lizzie Vega," she said, holding out her hand. "Sorry for interrupting."

"Not at all." Bobby shook her hand. "Bobby Doherty."

"Bobby takes care of things around here." Looking at her would be a mistake. The last thing he needed was to get tongue-tied in front of Bobby. "Keeps things running like a well-oiled machine."

"Really? That sounds like a lot of hard work." There was admiration in her voice.

"Never minded working hard." Bobby shrugged, his discomfort growing. "You do what needs doing, is all."

"I like that," Lizzie said. "That's a good life philosophy."

Bobby's chuckle was unexpected. "Well, I don't know about that." But he puffed up a little at her compliment.

Now she was charming Bobby. Dogs, babies, horses and his crusty foreman.

"I should get back to it. Work's not going to do itself, after all." Bobby nodded.

Hayden glanced at his watch. Weston would be

waking up soon. "I'll come back in a while—see what I can do."

"You give your little cowboy a big howdy from me." Bobby put his hat on and tipped it at Lizzie. "Weather report said more rain's expected this evening. Might be best to wait until it's all over—unless there's a whole fence down." Clipboard in hand, he headed toward the office.

More rain? Hayden glanced her way. Sure enough, her posture had gone ramrod stiff again. *Dammit.* "He liked you."

She took a deep breath and crossed her arms over her chest. "How could you tell?" She was staring at the open barn doors, wary.

A light breeze drifted through the open barn doors, lifting a few dark curls to dance around her cheek. His fingers itched to smooth them, to tuck them behind her ear, to draw her close… His throat felt tight. "I just can." He crouched, sucking air into his lungs as he gave Charley a firm rubdown. He knew Bobby's mention of rain was weighing on her—there'd been no missing her reaction. "It's Texas. Rain might just pass us by." He glanced at her, saw her nod, hugging herself tighter. "You okay, Lizzie?"

She nodded.

"You sure?" He stood, stepping closer to her. But he didn't touch her, didn't pull her against him and tell her everything would be okay.

Since he was blocking her view, she had no choice but to look up at him. And when her gaze collided with his…that tangible current electrified the space between them. His lungs were empty, aching for air.

She drew in an unsteady breath, her light hazel eyes searching his. "Yes. I'm sure."

He shoved his hands in his pockets, to stop himself from reaching for her. "Good."

"If you're needed here, I can watch Weston." There was a smile in her voice. "We had lots of fun this morning. He is the sweetest little man ever." Her genuine affection warmed him through. His son was his whole world. He was a good boy—his happy nature a constant reminder of all the good in life. "Or not, I just want to help…" She mumbled to a stop.

He cleared his throat, and forced himself to say, "I appreciate that."

"Hayden." She opened her mouth, then closed it— her hands flexing against her sides.

He waited, watching the shift of emotions on her face. Whatever she wanted to say, she was taking care to choose just the right words. Like it or not, he was bracing himself.

"I…" She shook her head. "Never mind."

He waited, hoping she'd change her mind. He might not like what she had to say, but he'd rather hear it. "You sure?"

"I… Sometimes I forget that I've only just met you." She winced. "And I realize that sounds strange—it *is* strange. But I understand why you'd be hesitant about me watching Weston. Why wouldn't you be? I'm practically a stranger."

He wasn't sure what he was expecting, but that wasn't it. If he was being honest with himself, he hadn't given a second thought to her caring for Weston. "Never crossed my mind." He shook his head. "Maybe it's wrong to put so much faith in dogs and children but…" He shrugged. "I trust Sierra's, Charley's and Weston's instincts. They're all at ease with you."

Lizzie was smiling now.

That smile tugged at his heart—something fierce.

The sky was endless blue. Every few steps along the path back to the house, she'd check again. Still blue—still cloudless. With any luck, Bobby's weather forecast was wrong. It could happen. Her luck had been improving. She considered herself extremely lucky to be here, safe, with Hayden and his family.

"Do you think the roads will be open tomorrow?" she asked, watching Sierra bound by, splashing through a puddle, then circling back for more. Charley followed, eagerly digging in the muddied water with his front paws—and splattering Sierra's white coat with sludge.

"Charley." Hayden's voice was stern, his finger-snap bringing both dogs to a standstill. "You two are a mess." And it only got worse when both dogs did a head-to-toe shake, then sat, watching him. There was mud dripping off Charley's muzzle and Sierra's white coat was speckled with mud and dirt, but they both looked so ashamed that Lizzie couldn't help but laugh.

"Looks like you're both getting a bath when we get back." Hayden sighed, but he was smiling when he looked at her. "Glad you think it's funny."

"I can't help it." She shrugged, still laughing. "They were so…so happy. You were having fun, weren't you?"

Sierra started wagging her tail, flinging mud in the process. Lizzie held up her arm, to shield herself, but not before she was thoroughly splattered.

"Is that a yes?" She shook off her hands and arms, still laughing.

Hayden reached over. "You've got something right there." He rubbed his thumb along her jaw.

One little touch and her focus narrowed in scope. Namely on Hayden. His light brown eyes sweeping her face. His fingers on her skin. The crooked grin on his mouth. His proximity made it impossible to see anything else.

"You've got some in your hair, too." He shook his head.

"I do?" She reached up, brushing her hair from her shoulders. "Guess I'm getting a bath, too." *What did I just say?* Her cheeks were burning. "Not by you…

Obviously." *Way to make it so much worse.* "I mean, I can take a *shower*, of course… Alone."

His crooked grin grew into a full-fledged smile. "I got it."

"Okay." Pure embarrassment had her picking up the pace. She wasn't sure which was worse, the extent to which she'd managed to make an idiot out of herself or her over-the-top reaction to…*him*. Either way, she breathed a sigh of relief when the house came into sight.

The back door opened and Jan came out, shielding her eyes. "Land sakes, what happened to you?"

Lizzie looked down at herself. "Sierra and Charley found a mud puddle."

"Did they ever." Jan shook her head. "Hayden James, they are not coming inside until—"

"I know, Mom." Hayden closed the gate behind them. "I'll take care of it. How are you feeling?"

"Almost human." Jan smiled. "I figured I'd peel myself out of the bed long enough to see what's what and go from there."

"I'm glad you're feeling a little better." Lizzie tucked her hair behind her ear, tugging a bit of mud from the long strands. The first time Jan had seen her, they were tangled up in a late-night kiss. Instead of making a better second impression, the woman got to see her covered in muck, with mud in her hair.

"Me, too." Jan gave her a head-to-toe inspection.

"I can find you some more clean clothes—let you get cleaned up."

"My clothes are probably dry by now." Lizzie shrugged, plucking the T-shirt away from her chest. "I'll wash these, I promise." She paused, looking back and forth between Hayden and his mother. "Do you need help with the dogs?"

"Hayden can take care of them, can't you, Hayden?" Jan asked.

"Yep." Hayden smiled at her, shaking his head after giving her pants another once-over.

"If you're sure?" she asked.

"I'm sure." He nodded.

"I'll be quick." She hurried into the shop, opened the mudroom door and tugged off her boots. She grabbed her clothes from the dryer, headed into the bathroom, kicked off her dirty clothes and hopped under the tepid stream of the shower. She didn't know how the whole generator situation worked but she didn't want to use up all the hot water. She was showered, dressed and carrying her clothes and towels to the washing machine in no time.

"You don't have to do that," Jan said. She sat at the kitchen table, a cup of tea, the baby monitor and a newspaper on the table before her.

"It's the least I can do." Lizzie loaded up the machine, added soap and started the cycle. "Thank you—for the clothes and the shelter and hospitality."

"You are most welcome." Jan smiled. "Weather like that makes travel a hazard."

Lizzie didn't argue. Of course, being terrified of rain didn't help. Once she started thinking about rain, Bobby's comment about the weather had her crossing the room to peer out the French doors. The sky was still brilliant blue—no clouds, no darkness, no hint of more rain headed this way. "Mr. Doherty mentioned we might be getting more rain."

"I wouldn't be surprised." Jan nodded. "I get an ache in my hip when it's going to rain. And it's aching."

Lizzie frowned but the telltale squeak of Weston's baby monitor provided the distraction she needed. "I can get him," she offered.

Jan nodded, her gaze warm upon Lizzie. "If you don't mind. I'm feeling better but I'd hate to get him sick."

"No, of course." Lizzie nodded and hurried down the hallway to Weston's nursery. She peeked inside and smiled. "Hello, handsome."

Weston had been holding on to the crib railing, one leg over the edge, but he stopped when she walked in—a huge smile on his face.

"I saw you trying to sneak out." She tapped his nose. "Who is the strongest little man? I think it's, let me see? Hmm, it's you, Weston."

"Da-ba-ba," Weston chattered back, adding a whole string of incoherent noises.

"You don't say?" she asked, lifting him from his crib. "I had no idea."

"Da da yum yum," Weston added, clapping his hands again.

"I am sure we can find your daddy and get you something yummy, too." She laid him on the changing table. "Let's get you all cleaned up and we'll go see what we can find, shall we?"

"Yum yum yum…" Weston said, smiling. He reached up, grabbing handfuls of her hair in his little fists.

"My hair is messy." She nodded, changing his diaper quickly. "But at least there's no mud in it anymore."

"Bla-ba-ba," Weston said, playing with her hair.

"It was very bla-ba-ba," she repeated, earning her a huge smile. "Ready?" She scooped him up and set him on his feet. "Ready, set, go."

He smiled up at her, then trotted out the door and down the hall. He paused at the top of the three steps that led into the open living space, waiting for her to take his hand before attempting to climb down.

"Happy to help," she said, letting him figure out the best way to take the three steps down into the great room. "I know you can do this, Weston. I believe in you."

Weston said, almost singing, "Da da da."

"Yes, we'll find Daddy, too," she promised, watching as he teetered on the first step, his hold tightening on hers. He took another step and stared up at her, looking frustrated. "One-two-three," she said, giving Weston an extra bounce on the final step. "You did it."

Weston smiled up at her.

"Yes, you should be proud of yourself." She nodded. "Well done."

His little head was tilted so far back to see her that he sat down, right there, on the floor.

"Are we done walking?" she asked, scooping him up and onto her hip. "That was a lot of work."

He patted her chest.

"You're welcome." She loved the way he rested his head against her shoulder. "Weston, oh my, you are a love." Hugging him close was the most natural thing in the world.

"Goodness, he's got you wrapped around his little finger," Jan said.

"He does indeed. But I did promise him a snack, so that might have something to do with it." Lizzie bounced Weston. "Isn't that right? Yum yum?"

Weston clapped his hands, then leaned forward, chanting, "Da da da da."

Hayden was standing in the doorway of the mudroom, running a towel over his head. "Hi, Weston." Hayden's voice was pitched low and gentle. There was something truly magnificent about the way this big, burly grown man lit up at the sight of his son.

"Da da," Weston repeated, clapping his hands and reaching for him.

"You want Daddy?" Lizzie asked, walking to Hayden.

Hayden's eyes met hers, all the warmth and affection and love he bore for his son shining in the depths of his gaze. Her poor heart almost combusted. It wasn't fair to react this way. She barely knew this man. She had no place here—she and Hayden Mitchell had no future. How could they? Her life was in Houston. It had taken time, determination and hard work to save for her garden home. Even more determination and endless hours to earn her position with the university. In time, her home would become a refuge and her job would bring her joy again. For now, well, she didn't want to think about her empty house or the stress of her job... Her life was in Houston, not here. His was here—with his family and the ranch.

Now if he'd only stop looking at her like that... like he might, possibly, be interested in her. It didn't matter that she liked the way he was looking at her. Or that, deep down, she didn't want him to stop looking at her that way. Not even the teeniest bit. *All* of this was temporary. It had to be. She sucked in a deep breath and tore her gaze from his. Of course, it was temporary. *Enough, Lizzie. Don't let your imagination go wild.*

Using words like *future* when it came to a man she'd known for less than two days was ridiculous.

Where had that come from? Why? *Because I've never felt this way before?* The thought popped out of nowhere, a hard truth Lizzie had been attempting to ignore.

When Hayden took Weston from her, the slight brush of his hand on hers sent a jolt of pure electricity from her fingertips down the length of her spine to settle, warm and tingly, in the pit of her stomach. *No. No.* This wasn't happening. She wasn't, couldn't, fall for Hayden Mitchell.

"Thank you," he said, bouncing Weston.

"Of course." She avoided looking at him. "What's for snack?" she asked, doing her best to shut down any further thoughts about the man standing before her. A man wearing a skintight shirt—stretched taut over the sort of chest and abdomen that she'd only ever seen in marble. *So much for not looking at him.*

"Did you see the school board approved the new high school?" Jan asked. "They're looking for new teachers and staff and planning all sorts of fancy bells and whistles for the place. I guess that's part of school these days. All the technology."

"About time." Hayden nodded. "If Granite Falls wants people to consider living here and commuting into San Antonio or Austin, they need to have good schools. And, yes, plenty of technology." He smiled at his mother.

"It's exciting." Jan smiled. "You ever think about teaching high school, Lizzie?"

Which was such an unexpected question, Lizzie wasn't sure what to say. "Well…"

"She's a professor." Hayden glanced her way. "I'm pretty sure a big-city university professor wouldn't think twice about moving to Granite Falls." Hayden's tone was almost…*dismissive*. Irritated, even.

Why? He had some ax to grind with big-city university professors? That seemed a little far-fetched. Was it because she'd never ridden a horse? He *had* seemed awfully troubled by that in the barn. She was perfectly capable of learning to ride—if she wanted to. Or he might just not like his mother's suggestion. Her moving here…teaching here. Was that it? She *had* freaked out, invaded his space and freaked out some more. He was irritated because he was ready for her to go home.

That made sense.

She risked a glance his way, surprised at the odd tightening in the pit of her stomach. What was that about? She had a life waiting for her. *It's not like I would ever move here.*

Besides, other than his work with veteran dogs, his adorable son and the fact he looked incredible in a cowboy hat, what did she really know about Hayden Mitchell? *That his kisses turn me to Jell-O.* She shook her head. *Not helping.*

Sierra sneezed, interrupting her odd train of thoughts. "Bless you," she said, earning a strange look from Jan, a smile from Hayden and a giggle from Weston.

While she made a piece of whole-wheat toast with peanut butter for Weston, Jan read the road alerts pinging on her phone out loud, and Hayden got Weston situated in the high chair.

"Looks like it's going to be late tomorrow afternoon at this rate," Jan said, shaking her head. "And that's if the rain stops."

"It might be best if you planned to stay through tomorrow night, Lizzie," Hayden said, securing a bib around Weston's neck. "It's hard to judge water depth once it gets dark."

The very idea of driving along dimly lit backcountry roads covered in water was like being plunged into ice. She started her breathing, concentrating on cutting the crusts from Weston's toast to keep all the memories rushing in from taking control. Yes, there were times she could still feel the water inching higher, still feel the brush and pull of whatever she couldn't see in the dark, rising water. Sometimes, she could almost hear Taffy's mournful whimpers and the torrential beat of the rain on the roof slowly cracking overhead. But her memories didn't paralyze her anymore. It wasn't always easy, but she had the tools to keep herself from spiraling now. She put the toast on a plate and carried it to the table, her gaze darting to the back window. Now her heart was racing, the pressure in her chest spreading rapidly.

"I appreciate the hospitality, truly. I hate to be an inconvenience…" Her forced laugh didn't fool anyone.

"Lizzie?" Jan was up, taking her hands in hers. "Your hands are freezing."

"I'm fine." She didn't sound fine. Her voice was high-pitched, more squeak than anything. She gently pulled her hands away, rubbing them together, and offered the woman what was likely a pathetic attempt at a smile.

"Are you sure?" Jan asked. "You're white as a sheet."

Lizzie nodded, not trusting her voice. As long as she didn't look out the back window, she *would* be fine. She picked up an apple and crossed the kitchen. All she needed was a few seconds to collect herself— just a few. Sierra appeared at her side, leaning against Lizzie's calf. It helped, some. But there was no steadying her heart rate or the ache in her lungs. Not now that the sky had gone from brilliant blue to gray.

Chapter Ten

Hayden filled the generator with gas, secured the shop door and flipped off the lights before heading back inside the house. He lingered, appreciating the view. Lizzie and Weston were on a play mat on the floor, stacking a tower of large plastic blocks and knocking them down with glee. Every time Weston knocked the tower over, Lizzie clapped and cheered with the same enthusiasm as the last time. It was no wonder his son—what had his mother said?—had Lizzie wrapped around his little finger. He didn't blame his son for wanting to win Lizzie over. Damn it all, he felt the same way about the woman. With her, he seemed to be lacking his go-to rationality.

It was like she short-circuited his brain, putting his wants and needs and feelings above reason and logic. That, for him, was a first. He wasn't sure what to do with it, with her—with any of this.

Charley and Sierra were lying in front of the French doors, a pile of fur and snores.

"There's Daddy," Lizzie said, holding Weston's hands so he could stand. "Say hi, Weston."

"Da da da." Weston singsonged, bouncing as he did so.

"Hi, Weston." He waved. "Where did Grandma go?"

"She headed back to bed." Lizzie frowned. "She said she's still not feeling one hundred percent."

He sighed, rubbing his nose. "I thought I smelled more Lysol." He noticed the newspaper on the counter—open to the employment section. There, in black-and-white, was the list of openings for the new Granite Falls High School. His mother had circled them with a yellow highlighter. *Subtle, Mom.* He glanced at Lizzie.

"She might have sprayed every surface with her antibacterial spray first." Lizzie nodded, smiling.

He blinked, blindsided as always by the force of her smile. So far, the darkening sky was the only real transformation outside. He hoped that was the extent of it. He was enjoying her smile far too much to have a storm system steal it away. Not just her smile—but her spirit. This Lizzie, full of smiles and laughter and energy, was a completely different person from the one he'd met.

"Ba ma la la," Weston said, smiling back and forth between the two of them.

"Translation?" Hayden asked her.

"I think he was reminding me to ask you about the pictures." Head cocked to the side, she asked, "Is that it, Weston?"

Weston clapped his hands.

She nodded. "Yes, that's it."

Hayden had to laugh then, earning him a fleeting glance from Lizzie. It wasn't his imagination—he knew it. She'd been avoiding eye contact since she'd carried Weston in from his nap. The question was, why?

She stood, letting Weston hold on to her fingers, and walked slowly across the room—to the gallery of family photos on the far wall. "Are these all the Mitchells?" she asked. "I'm guessing these two are your brothers."

"They are." He joined her, staring at the picture of the three of them. "Kyle and John."

"Leaving a trail of broken hearts wherever you go, I'm guessing." She shook her head.

He frowned, looking at her. "Why is that?"

"You're all incredibly good-looking." She looked at him like he was growing a second head.

"I'm incredibly good-looking?" he asked, watching her cheeks bloom red. *Interesting.*

"I… Well…" She sighed, beyond flustered. "Isn't it obvious? Are you fishing for compliments, Hayden Mitchell?" Her long braid fell forward, hanging over her shoulder. "Who is that?"

"My father." He stared at the picture of his family— one of the last they'd taken before his father's death. "Pete Mitchell."

"I thought so. There's a strong father-son resemblance."

"He was a good-looking man, too?" he asked, laughing at the scowl she sent his way. "He was a good man. A good father." He sighed. "He died when I was sixteen. There's not a day that goes by that I don't miss him." Which was more than he'd planned to share, true or not.

"I'm sorry." She crouched, Weston leaning against the wall to look up at them both. But it was Lizzie's warm gaze that held his attention. The flash of pain and sympathy on her face touched him. "Truly."

Weston chose that moment to turn, throw his little arms around Lizzie and press an openmouthed kiss to her cheek.

"Goodness." Lizzie's smile was blinding as she pulled Weston into a big hug. "I don't know where that came from but thank you."

Weston patted on her shoulders, one hand twining in the hair that had slipped free of her braid.

"Is my hair still messy?" she asked.

"No." He hadn't meant to answer. Or say a damn

thing. But he had. One gruff word that drew her wide-eyed gaze his way. And there, in those eyes, he caught a glimpse of the same heat, the same fire, that he'd tasted in her kiss the night before. His response was instantaneous. He couldn't fight the magnetic pull between them if he'd wanted to.

He didn't want to.

With a deep, wavering breath, she picked up Weston and turned, heading back to the play mat and mountain of toys. Weston sat, chattering away at his books and toys and Lizzie, too. She sat on the edge of the blanket, carefully avoiding his gaze once more. "What do your brothers do?" she asked.

"Kyle is air force, active. John's a marine." He still wondered if his little brother had chosen a different branch purely to get under Hayden's skin. He'd denied it, of course. But he had said it was the only way to ensure Hayden didn't interfere with his career.

"You must worry about them." She continued to stack up the blocks. "How often do you get to see one another?"

He stared at the picture, the smiles… When had they last been together? "It's been a year?" That sounded about right. "A few weeks before Weston was born." By then, he and Karla had already begun talking about a divorce and their path forward. His brothers had rallied, giving him the strength and support he needed to come to terms with the changes his new world would demand of him. And, after those four days of solidarity, he'd hoped it was the beginning of a new relationship with his brothers—especially John. But, once the weekend was over and his brothers had returned to their posts, communication had become less and less frequent.

"They've never met him?"

He turned. "No."

Her brows rose as she regarded Weston. "Well, little man, you just wait. When you do get to meet your uncles, you will win them over. You'll see."

Weston kicked out and giggled, sending the blocks all over.

"Exactly, it's very exciting." Lizzie laughed, up on her hands and knees collecting the blocks again.

He helped with the block collection and sat on the opposite side of the mat, leaning back against the couch and stretching his legs out. There wasn't enough space to diffuse the electric spark between them but he was beginning to think *enough space* didn't exist.

Weston stood and carried some blocks to him. "Da da." He was so proud of himself he started clapping.

"Thank you." Hayden smiled, giving his son a thumbs-up. "Good job, Weston."

"Goo ja," Weston repeated.

"That's right." Hayden was laughing then. "Good job."

Weston was clapping so hard, he teetered back and sat down hard.

It was only when Hayden had stopped laughing that he realized it was raining. No thunder or lightning, not yet anyway, but the steady beat of a heavy rain on the roof overhead was unmistakable. Lizzie glanced up, her posture tightening as she curled in on herself. As if on cue, Sierra got up from her spot on the floor, crossed to Lizzie and flopped down against her side.

Lizzie smiled, resting one hand on Sierra's back. "She knows?"

Hayden watched the exchange, heartened by Lizzie's response. She wasn't holding her breath or counting. Sierra's weight, her presence, was giving Lizzie the reassurance she needed. "She's a smart dog."

"How do you think she knows?"

"Your heartbeat. Probably your respiration rate." He watched Lizzie's hand, and the way her fingers splayed to ruffle Sierra's coat.

"I'm glad she's the only one who can hear that." Lizzie's smile was forced, more sad than anything.

He studied her, so long and hard she had to know it. If she did, she didn't acknowledge it—or look at him. "If you want to talk about what happened, Lizzie—"

She was looking at him then. "I *know* I've dumped enough on you already, Hayden. I just… Well, it's a place I don't want to visit again. I mean, I do—with my therapist. But, outside of her office?" She broke off, shrugging. "I don't know if that makes any sense or not—"

"It does." He spun one of the blocks in his hands, considering his options. "I have a few of those. Places—memories—so deep and dark you can get lost in them."

Her nod was slow, wary.

"Charley helps me with that." Hayden smiled as Charley popped up and trotted to his side. "Don't you?"

Charley leaned into his touch, an appreciative rumble deep in his throat.

"Did you talk to someone? A counselor or therapist or something?" she asked, continuing to run her hand along Sierra's back.

"Mark Sai." He smiled. "Before he retired, I spent time on his couch, regularly. He was the one who had to clear us to return to our units—back to active duty. There are things you can't unsee—can't undo. Losing part of your team, worrying over civilians in the crossfire, losing a dog…" He patted Charley. "After a while, it takes a toll."

Head shaking, she covered her face with her hands. "You've been through all of that and you're still functioning." Her sharp intake of breath cut deep. "What's wrong with me?"

* * *

Lizzie was doing her best to keep it together. Hayden Mitchell knew what trauma was—*real* trauma—and yet he'd moved to her side and drawn her into his arms to comfort *her*.

"There's nothing wrong with you." His voice was soft.

"You've seen the way I react." She couldn't stop herself from burying her face against his chest.

His hands were firm against her back, rubbing up and down.

"I guess I should be happy I don't live in Oregon or Washington State. I'd never survive all the rain." It wasn't a very successful attempt at a joke.

His arms tightened. "If you were there, I'd never have met you." The words hung in the air—a mere whisper.

She looked up at him then, surprised, her heart hammering away. It was wrong to read more into what he'd just said but she couldn't help it. Storm aside, being stranded aside, she was happy she'd met him. And being here, with him and Weston, had made her happier than she'd been in... She couldn't remember the last time she was this happy. His words made her hope, with all her heart, he *wasn't* all that eager to see her leave. Maybe he was happy she was here, too. Happy enough that he'd bend his head and press his lips to hers. She ached for that—for him. If she thought her heart had been racing before, she'd been wrong.

His eyes were warm on her face. Warm and intent, concerned and soulful… And blazing. He was staring at her mouth then, his jaw tightening. "If you keep looking at me like that, I'm going to be making more apologies."

"I don't want your apologies," she whispered.

He swallowed, one hand sweeping the hair from her shoulder. "What do you want, Lizzie?"

To breathe. To think. To hold on to him and kiss him until—

"Da da," Weston said, resting one hand on each of them. "Ba ba da mim," he added, holding out a block.

Lizzie smiled, her gaze still caught up in Hayden's.

His crooked grin appeared, his thumb tracing along her jaw and making her light-headed before he turned to his son.

What was happening? Why was she so…so overwhelmed by this man? Then again, why shouldn't she be? She hadn't been kidding when she'd compared him to a knight in shining armor. She didn't know everything about him, but what she did know? As far as she was concerned, being a single father, rancher, veteran, champion of dogs and all-around decent human being totally equated to modern knighthood.

"Goo ja," Weston said again, with such enthusiasm Lizzie had to give him her full attention.

"Yes, Weston. You're quite the builder." She held

out her hands to him, nodding. "Come here. I know you can do it." She paused, glancing at Hayden. "He was trying to climb out of his crib. I meant to tell you earlier."

"He was?" Hayden asked. "I guess I need to lower his mattress."

Weston deposited the blocks in her lap and went back for another load, the concentration on his face beyond priceless.

She smiled. "I thought you'd want to know."

"I appreciate it." His voice was all low rumbles again.

Every nerve tingled, a flare of heat burning in her stomach. She was doing her best not to stare at Hayden when Weston dropped another load of blocks in her lap and fell forward into her hold with a joyous giggle.

She wrapped him up in a hug. "Are you sharing with me?" She tickled his sides, smiling at Weston's delighted laughter. "Something tells me you're going to be keeping your daddy on his toes in no time."

"I'm not sure I'm ready for this." Hayden chuckled.

"I'm pretty sure you don't have a choice." She glanced his way, still giving Weston a tickle-hug. It was the look on his face that made her stop. Specifically, the way he was looking at her. But Weston did his best to win her over, twining his arms around her neck and giving her a big kiss on the cheek. "Sweet kisses, Weston." She hugged him tight. "Thank you."

"Tan too," Weston repeated.

Hayden chuckled. "First *good job*, now *thank you*." He sighed. "Walking and talking?"

"Tan too," Weston said. "Yum yum."

Lizzie glanced at the clock. "Dinnertime?" Her attention was then sidetracked by the rain. How had she forgotten? It wasn't like she couldn't hear it, pounding away overhead.

Hayden stood and headed into the kitchen. "My boy lives by his stomach."

She stood, swinging Weston up into her arms, and followed Hayden into the kitchen, Sierra trailing after them. If she focused all of her energy on Weston and Hayden and dinner, maybe she could ward off her panic. Maybe? Sierra pressed her nose against Lizzie's palm, offering her support. *I can do this.* She gave Sierra an ear rub. *I'm game to try.*

Hayden opened the fridge, frowned and stepped back.

"French toast?" she asked, peering around him. "It's one of my specialties. That's easy and I bet this little guy would gobble it up. It's fast, too. If you have bread."

Hayden got the bread out of the pantry and took Weston so she could make dinner. She made a tall stack of French toast, sliced up some berries and bananas, and found some strawberry yogurt and the syrup.

"You look pretty at ease in my kitchen." Hayden took the bowl of berries she passed his way.

"Cooking is second nature. It's relaxing." She shrugged. "It's my grammy's love language— gathering in the kitchen to talk and cook and eat. I guess it's mine, too."

His fork paused, midway to his mouth. "Is this her recipe? If it is, I need to thank her."

"Yes. Complete with her top-secret ingredient." She smiled. "That's what makes it so yum yum."

Weston nodded.

"Grammy would *adore* you," she said to Weston, tapping his little nose.

"No more calling in the National Guard to rescue you?" he asked, taking another big bite of his dinner.

"I didn't say she'd like you." She pointed at him with her fork. "Just Weston."

Weston nodded again.

"But she might like you." She studied him. "You did take me in when I'd have been stranded on the side of the road."

"Walt might take offense to having his Quik N' Go being compared to the side of the road." He shrugged, the corner of his mouth kicking up. "Besides, if I'd left you there, who'd have helped me with Weston—with my mother sick?"

"Oh, I see." She cut up a few more pieces of toast

and put them on Weston's tray. "That's why you brought me here?"

He shoved a large bite of French toast into his mouth and shrugged.

"You see that, Weston?" she asked the baby. "Your daddy is picking on me. Here I thought it was my wit and charm that brought out his chivalrous side."

Hayden's brow cocked up but his mouth was too full to comment.

"Really, it's my ability to cook and change diapers?" She laughed when Weston nodded. "Well, I guess they're useful skills and, at this rate, I need to start exploring my backup plan. Nanny and chef, huh?" She was only partly kidding. If she couldn't get herself back on track, she'd lose her position at the university. If she did, then what?

"Why do you need a backup plan?" Hayden asked, adding three more slices of French toast to his plate. "Mark said you've been a professor for a couple of years."

They'd talked about her? "What else did he tell you?" She heard the brittle edge to her voice—so did he.

He leaned forward. "Nothing, Lizzie. That was it. I promise." He held his hands up, concerned. "Mark and I are friends, but he'd never betray a patient's confidence."

"I'm not his patient, exactly." She poked at her toast. "The university brought him in immediately after the hurricane, a sort of mental-health triage until long-term arrangements could be made for those of us who needed it. Dr. Sai referred me to Dr. Peeler, who's wonderful. And he sent me to you so…" She paused. "I'm very thankful for him."

"Did the hurricane damage the campus?" he asked, cutting his toast into smaller pieces.

"No." She rested her elbows on the table. "The campus was untouched." Her gaze darted to the window behind Hayden. *Only rain. That's all.* Sierra, who'd been lying on the floor by her chair, rested her paw on Lizzie's foot. "But, yes, I've been at the university for a while as a professor." She shrugged. "I also teach classes at the senior community center and the nearby after-school program."

"Because you like to stay busy." Hayden nodded.

"I do." She smiled. "And I love sharing art, the joy of art, with people. Of all ages. I bet Weston here would love to play with paint. Or mash his fingers in some clay. Wouldn't you?"

"Can you teach classes at schools and senior centers as a job?" Hayden asked. "If you decide not to go back to the university, I mean?" He smiled slowly. "I was paying attention."

"A little too well… I could. Maybe. But I love my job—I used to love my job. I worked so hard to get it." He didn't need to know that the university might decide not to have her back. "I'm just… I'm not sure what to do."

"Tan too," Weston said, patting his tray.

"More?" Lizzie cut up another piece of toast. "Glad you like it, Weston," she said, placing the bite-size pieces on his tray.

Weston nodded, eating another bite before yawning.

"Like clockwork." Hayden glanced at the clock on the wall.

Last night she'd been too worked up over the weather to contemplate being alone with Hayden. Tonight… Well, it was only rain. If Jan was correct, the roads would keep her here one more night. That was all she had. One more night than she'd thought. She hadn't expected to feel so…relieved she wasn't leaving. Tonight and tomorrow and then she'd head back to Houston.

Houston.

The university.

Her empty house.

Her life.

Well, what was left of it…

The thought of leaving caused a hollow ache to form, gnawing at the base of her stomach. And since she wasn't ready to consider *why* she was having such a strong reaction to returning to the real world, she decided not to think about it. Not yet, anyway.

She smiled at Weston, who was rubbing his eyes. "Tired out?" she asked. "All that walking will do that."

"Guess it's bath time, then bed." Hayden stood, lifting Weston from the high chair. "I'll clean up the kitchen after he's in bed."

"I don't mind." She stood, already stacking the plates.

"I do." His hand rested on her forearm. "I didn't bring you out here to wait on me and my son."

"I know that." She smiled, the warmth of his hand on her arm triggering all sorts of interesting tingles. "But it gives me something to do." She pointed at the window, hoping that was explanation enough.

"Meaning you're going to do it anyway?"

"Well…" She smiled. "Yes. I am."

He grinned.

That grin. She drew in an unsteady breath. "After this little cutie is in bed, what's the plan?" She smiled at Weston, his head resting against Hayden's chest— his eyelids heavy. "A game of chess? Or a movie? Or…" *Something.* Her gaze slid up—to Hayden's face. And that grin. *Definitely need to find* something *to do.* Otherwise the pure temptation of Hayden Mitchell's smile would be impossible to resist. *Stop staring at his mouth.*

"I guess now is as good a time as ever to talk about Sierra. I've made my decision." Hayden's jaw muscle clenched just enough to catch her eye. "I'll be back." He carried Weston down the hall, leaving Lizzie to wonder what, exactly, his decision was.

His voice was gruff… Not at all the way a person sounded before delivering good news. As usual, her imagination went the worst-case-scenario route. Hayden was going to tell her Sierra wasn't going home with her. He'd be polite—he couldn't risk her falling apart again. *Of course, the answer was no.* If it was a yes, he'd have smiled. Wouldn't he? And he hadn't. She worried she was too broken for Sierra. Still, her brain continued to work through things to say that might change his mind. Not once, the entire time she was straightening the kitchen or washing the dishes, did she pause long enough to notice the rain had kicked up and, in the distance, thunder was rolling in.

Chapter Eleven

Hayden smoothed the blanket over Weston and crept from the nursery, closing the door behind him with care. It had been a big day. Weston was adding new words thanks to Lizzie's encouragement and coaxing.

Lizzie. The woman had a powerful effect on him. And he had no idea what he should do about it. *There is nothing to do.* As much as he'd come to admire her, he knew their paths would lead them separate ways. Even if he was drawn to her—her spirit and charm, strength and laughter—there was no point in dwelling on something that couldn't be. Instead, he'd be thankful for the encouragement she was giving his boy. She'd given Weston so much confidence.

Now it was Hayden's turn to return the favor.

It wasn't easy to come back from a trauma. The mind was a powerful thing. Once a person was that shaken, it was hard to trust yourself again. But Hayden knew Lizzie was ready. With Sierra's help, she'd be back on her own two feet. After watching the two of them together, it had been clear he had no say-so in the choice. Sierra already thought Lizzie was hers. Now Lizzie needed to know that—to make it official.

A quick search showed the kitchen was neat as a pin.

And empty.

No Lizzie.

He frowned and turned slowly.

Where was she?

He'd been a little too aware of the way she was staring at his mouth to give her the appropriate reassurance. What had he said, exactly? All of his focus had been on not pulling her into his arms. *Way to go, jackass.* He sighed, headed back down the hall and knocked, softly, on her door.

No answer—the only sound was the rain beating down on the roof.

Was that it? Had leaving her alone with the storm brewing sent her into hiding? If he'd been thinking about her well-being versus the feel of her lips against his, he wouldn't have made such a mistake. He shook his head, feeling like an ass. The last thing he wanted was to compound her stress. Their time was running out. The thought of her leaving… Well, he wanted to make the most of what little time they had left together. There was no ignoring the tightness in his chest.

He knocked again, then gripped either side of the door frame, that creeping tension pressing against his chest as a dozen things to say or do flitted through his brain. Some of which scared the shit out of him. The best way to start? "Lizzie, I'm sorry." He cleared his throat. "I guess I got sidetracked…" *Trying not to pull you close.* "With Weston's routine." Which was a damn lie. "And I didn't think about the rain. Or leaving you on your own. So…" He shook his head. "I'm sorry."

"No worries," Lizzie said.

He spun to find her standing at the end of the hall, a hesitant smile on her face and a stack of folded laundry in her arms. Charley and Sierra were flanking her and—maybe he was imagining it but—all three of them were giving him an odd look. Lizzie was rubbing off. Next, he'd be believing Sierra *was* smiling. He sucked in a deep breath. "Hey." *Real smooth, Hayden, real smooth.*

"Laundry." She held up the stack of laundry. "The borrowed clothes. All clean and dry."

"Keeping busy." He shook his head.

"You're catching on." She pushed the braid from her shoulder. "Besides, if you think I'm okay with you cleaning up after me, when you've been so kind, you'd be wrong. The least I can do is clean up my own messes—so let me, please." She shrugged. "Where should I put this?"

It was easy to get caught up in how animated she was when she spoke. If she wasn't holding freshly laundered clothes, he knew she'd be using her hands. It made him smile. "Might as well hold on to them—since the news says things won't be clearing up tomorrow." He pushed off the door frame to let her pass.

She carried everything into her room, set it on the dresser and turned to face him. "So, I have a pretty good idea what you've decided about Sierra…" Her gaze darted from him to Sierra. "Can I just say that I understand why you'd say no—"

"You do?" he interrupted.

"Of course I do. I know my behavior has been… *odd*. I understand why you'd think I'd be too much work for Sierra." She was staring up at him then, wide-eyed.

"You think so?" There was a sheen to her eyes—tears? His chest tightened and he cleared his throat. "Hold on, Lizzie—"

"No, you hold on." She stood straight, her chin wavering. "I *am* a lot of work." She shrugged, shaking her head. "*You* said she and I connected. And we have. That counts for something, doesn't it? And I will take care of her."

He didn't argue. "I know that."

But she didn't seem to hear him because she kept on talking. "And while I might be a lot of work, she will get something out of this partnership, too." She blinked once. Then again. Her indrawn breath was a shudder. "She'll get me, Hayden. And all my love. Every day—I promise. And I promise, I will take the very best care of her." Her cheeks were dark red.

"I know." He nodded.

"You do?" She blinked rapidly, surprised—a single tear tracking down her cheek. "Really?"

"She picked you. For me, that's answer enough." He couldn't stand it any longer. After a brief hesitation, he stroked the tear from her cheek with the pad of his thumb.

"You seemed so…" Lizzie swallowed, sniffing, her hazel eyes searching his. "Angry? *Something.* Not happy. *Not* like you were going to tell me Sierra was coming home with me, at least."

"I'm not angry." Not at her. Maybe, a little, with himself—for reacting to her the way he did.

"So, she's mine?" The question was a whisper. "And I'm hers?"

He nodded.

And Lizzie's smile tore at the restraint slipping from his control. It all but disappeared when she stepped forward to hug him. "Thank you, Hayden."

He didn't stop himself then. He wrapped her up in his arms and held her against him. What could it hurt? For a few minutes, anyway? But the sudden tug in his chest told him differently. This would hurt. Her leaving. He sighed, letting go and stepping back. "Good?"

She nodded, smiling so sweetly his arms ached to pull her close again. "Now I have to do something to thank you."

That smile was as bright and warm as the sun. The tug was harder now, the warning undeniable. "Nope." He shook his head, the guest bedroom shrinking around them. "So…" He cleared his throat and turned, heading out of her bedroom and back into the living room, sucking air into his lungs.

Lizzie and Sierra were right behind him, the bounce in Lizzie's step unmistakable. "I told her." Lizzie said. "I think she's happy, too."

"Is she smiling again?" Hayden teased.

"Yes." Lizzie frowned at him. "Look at her, Hayden. How can you not see it?" She crouched by Sierra. "See?" She stared up at him.

"I guess she does look happy," he said, Lizzie's answering smile making the tug harder this time. Impossible to dismiss. *Dammit.*

"I was thinking…" Lizzie stood before him, too close for his liking. Yet, not close enough. "What if I bake some cinnamon rolls for breakfast? I make a mighty mean cinnamon roll. Unless you had something else in mind, of course." She paused. "I can make them, I mean. I'm sure you have important ranchy things to do."

"Ranchy, huh?" He chuckled. "I have work I could do." He always did.

"Okay." Was she disappointed or was he only imagining it? "Well, then, you get to work and I'll get to baking."

With a sigh, he headed to the desk on the far side of the living room. From the leather chair, he had a perfect view of the kitchen. And Lizzie.

He clicked on the computer and waited, his gaze shifting from the monitor to the woman twisting her hair up into a knot on the top of her head. The spreadsheet, line after line of numbers, filled the screen—but he was too distracted by Lizzie, humming, flitting around the kitchen. She hit a high note, then winced—glancing his way. Their gazes locked and, if it wasn't for the deep red staining her cheeks, he would have laughed.

"Sorry," she whispered. "I get a little carried away."

"Don't let me stop you." He cleared his throat.

For ten minutes, he stared at the same five columns of numbers. He tried, he did, but she was humming and dancing—even both dogs were watching. Eventually he gave up. There was no point. He wasn't getting a thing done. Except for staring at Lizzie, that is. He stood, stretched and headed back to the kitchen.

Her gaze met his. "Done?"

"Yep." *No.* Not in the least. "Need help?"

"Sure." She nodded, the knot on her head sliding to one side. "I need a pan."

Hayden found a pan, sprayed it with no-stick spray and set it on the marble countertop. "Next?"

"Mix this?" She handed him a bowl.

"Can do." He mixed, glad that his presence hadn't stopped her humming. Off-key or not, he liked it. It was very...Lizzie. "Anything else?"

Her brows rose. "You're very goal oriented, aren't you?"

"Guess so." He watched as she kneaded the dough, her fingers coated in flour, cinnamon and sugar crystals. "Growing up out here, there wasn't time for wasting. If you were doing something, there was a reason for it. Means I'm no good at downtime—"

"I might know a little something about that myself." Her smile was bright now—like the sun.

"I guess you do." He paused, his gaze traveling over her face.

Her gaze fell from his about the time her cheeks flushed a deep red again.

He cleared his throat, his gaze hanging on the streak of flour along the side of her neck. "What else can I do?"

"Nothing." She shrugged, her gaze darting to the window. "Talk to me?" There was the slightest waver in her voice.

He'd been so caught up in her that he'd missed the flicker in the sky. "I can do that." He wasn't known for being the talkative type but, for Lizzie, he'd give it a go. She used the back of her hand to smooth a curl from her forehead, leaving more flour. "You and Weston have more and more in common."

"We do?" She blew the same curl aside and peered at him. "Do tell." She rolled the dough out with ease. "I can't wait to hear this." She blew the same curl again.

He reached up, tucking the curl into the knot on top of her head. He was proud of himself for resisting the urge to pull her hair free and run his fingers through the silky-soft curls. "You both like to laugh. You're busy. Talk a lot. Make messes. Sing songs and like dogs." He swallowed as her gaze locked with his. "And apple pie…" More than that, when they—she and Weston—smiled, Hayden smiled, too. Their happiness demanded he feel the same. And, when he was with them—either of them—he was content. More than that: he was whole.

"Considering I think Weston is pretty awesome company, I'm fine having things in common with him. But, I'm pretty sure the two of us aren't the only ones who like those things." There was no denying the growing tension between them. The longer he stared at her, the harder it was to think or feel or see anything else. Just Hayden, holding the baking pan, looking out of sorts and far too handsome for his own good. She swallowed. "As you said, who doesn't like apple pie?" She shrugged. "And I might make messes, but I always clean up after myself. *Always.*" A clap of thunder overhead had the rolling pin falling from her hand to the floor. It hit the floor, leaving a halo of flour all over the cool surface. "See… I'll clean that up." She turned on the faucet and reached for the kitchen rag.

His hand clasped her wrist. "It will wait."

"No." She wriggled free. "I'll get it."

Another clap of thunder—this time rattling the window.

She ran the rag under the warm water, squeezed out the excess and knelt on the ground to wipe up the flour. But there was no way she could focus on cleanup with the rain pounding on the roof, followed by a sudden burst of thunder.

Sierra walked across the floor, pressing her wet nose against Lizzie's side. With her broad head, she nudged until Lizzie was sitting on the floor. Sierra slid onto the floor and rested her head in Lizzie's lap. Those big chocolate brown eyes bore into her own, searching and offering all the reassurance in the world. When the windows rattled again, Lizzie gave up and leaned back against the wooden cabinets. Sierra was doing whatever she could to make Lizzie feel better. And, weird or not, sitting on Hayden's kitchen floor with Sierra's head in her lap *was* making her feel better.

"It's just thunder, right?" She scratched Sierra behind the ear.

Sierra's lids drooped but her gaze never slipped. Those chocolate brown eyes stayed entirely fixed on Lizzie—until Lizzie's heartbeat slowed and it was easier to breathe. Then, Sierra leaned into her touch and offered her a soft doggie groan of appreciation.

From the corner of her eye, she saw Hayden sit on the opposite side of the kitchen floor. His long legs stretched out along her side. Charley took that moment to hop across Lizzie and Sierra to sprawl alongside Hayden.

"Well," Lizzie said.

Hayden gave Charley's side a pat. "Well."

"Nice floors." She tried to tease, wincing when the lights flickered overhead.

"They are." Hayden nodded. "I helped lay the tiles. It's work to get the angle right."

Lizzie actually looked at the tiles then. "I bet." Another clap of thunder and she sank both hands into Sierra's thick fur. The steady beat of Sierra's heart beneath her palms gave Lizzie something to focus on—something other than the thunder and shaking glass and flickering lights overhead.

Sierra looked up at her, those brown eyes so intent it was like the dog was reading her mind. "You said it. She can hear my heart rate." She glanced at

Hayden—her heart twisting at the concern lining his handsome face. "Which, as you've probably guessed, is at rabbit speed."

He grinned. "Rabbit speed?"

"Fast." She explained. "A rabbit's normal is between one hundred and twenty and one hundred and fifty beats per minute. A human heart rate is around seventy to one hundred."

His grin was huge now. "And you know this because…"

"Oh, I had a rabbit when I was younger. My great-aunt's neighbor was moving and couldn't take her rabbit so I inherited him." She shrugged. "He was adorable. Newton. He was black-and-white with floppy ears. He loved animal crackers. He'd play fetch with a ball."

"One twenty to one fifty beats, huh? Your heart is beating that fast?" He shook his head.

"I'm fine." She sighed, running Sierra's velvety-soft ear between her fingers and thumb. "I am fine. If you…don't want to sit on your kitchen floor, you don't have to. Not on my account." Something told her Hayden didn't make a habit of sitting on the kitchen floor. It was sweet. *And I'm pathetic.* "Sierra will stay with me."

"Charley's comfortable now." He patted Charley's side, smiling her way.

The moment their gazes collided, a gentle warmth washed over her. It was different this time. She still ached for him but this…this *feeling* didn't set her blood on fire. This was like a tether—a life preserver to keep her afloat. Something to cling to. How could something so new feel so…right? So secure?

"You okay, Lizzie?" Hayden asked, his leg moving closer to touch hers.

She blinked, unable to break the hold of his gaze. "I'm okay," she whispered, wishing that was true. *How was this okay?* A person didn't develop feelings for someone they barely knew. Not in real life. *That's silly.*

But… How else could she explain what was happening? Because, right or wrong, she was definitely feeling all sorts of things for this man. Honest-to-goodness actual feelings that were both terrifying and delightful. *What is wrong with me?*

The sudden burst of thunder was so loud—so close—Lizzie jumped. In seconds, she'd pulled her knees to her chest, hugging them close, her forehead resting on them. Sierra was up, sticking her nose beneath her arms. Lizzie's grip eased, draping one arm around the dog's shoulders.

There was a general scuffling and the click of dog paws on tile flooring. When stillness resumed, she peered through one eye to find Hayden sitting next to her. Shoulder to shoulder. Pressed close, his scent a welcome distraction. He tilted his head back, resting it on the cabinet door behind them. He almost looked at ease. Almost. If his jaw muscle wasn't clenched tight and his lips weren't pressed flat and his eyes weren't closed, that is.

"Sorry. That one was…loud. I'm fine. Really." She blew out a slow, unsteady breath and did her best to smile at him.

"I know you'll probably say no, but if you want to talk…" Hayden glanced her way. "I'll listen."

She rested her cheek on her knees and looked his way. He meant it, she could tell. "Why?" The question slipped out. But now, it was out there. One word, hanging between them.

His eyes narrowed slightly, the muscle in his jaw bulging once more. From the pensive furrow of his brow, he seemed to be considering his words. When his brow smoothed, he said, "I just…do." His gaze swept over her face, one hand running along the back of his neck. "Sometimes dragging the ghosts that haunt us into the light steals some of their power."

She was staring at him, then. His words resonated—deeply.

"I'll sit here with you, face them with you." He shrugged. "If you want."

"Yes." She swallowed, surprised by her answer. But then the words started coming and there was no stopping them. "Mrs. Lawrence has a little white dog, a mop really, named Taffy. Mrs. Lawrence is my neighbor…was my neighbor." She drew in a deep breath. "Taffy was an escape artist. Little enough to squeeze between the fence posts and fast enough that Mrs. Lawrence, at well over eighty years old, couldn't catch her. When Taffy escaped, which was often, Mrs. Lawrence would call me." She slid closer to him, so close that when her legs rested on the tile floor there was no space between them.

Hayden shifted a bit, one arm draped across his lap, his hand within reach—if she wanted it.

"I was at work when Mrs. Lawrence called—she didn't like many people. A bit of a curmudgeon. Anyway, she'd fallen and she refused to call the paramedics because she knew she wasn't really hurt and could I come get her. I tried to tell her about the hurricane, that she needed to call for help, but she started crying. She never cried, ever."

He nodded.

"I drove home as quickly as I could." She drew in another deep breath. "I could tell she'd hurt herself. She couldn't get out of bed. I called the paramedics and they came but Taffy refused to come out. The paramedics were understandably anxious to get on their way so I promised her I'd get Taffy and follow behind. Taffy didn't want to cooperate."

Sierra was up, licking her fingers, tail wagging. Lizzie relaxed some, one hand sinking into Sierra's soft fur.

"I couldn't leave the dog. She is everything to Mrs. Lawrence. I mean, she has a son, but she prefers Taffy." Her laugh was forced.

Hayden's gaze met hers. "You stayed?"

"I did… In no time, water was sliding in under the door…rising. I kept chasing Taffy, which probably didn't help… Then she ran into the pantry." If it hadn't been for her sessions with Dr. Peeler, Lizzie would be falling apart right about now. She'd be back there—back in that pantry. "It was so dark and cold. I'd never felt so afraid. Or alone."

But I'm not alone. Unlike Charley, who was snoring and draped across Hayden, Sierra fixed her large brown eyes on Lizzie. Watching her. Protecting her. Steadying her. There for her. She ran a hand over Sierra's broad head and sighed. *I've got you, now, don't I?* She smiled. *We have each other.*

She'd been so caught up in Sierra that the warm roughness of Hayden's touch startled her. But the moment his fingers threaded with hers, the way he rested her hand in his lap, captured her full attention.

Chapter Twelve

Hayden could almost see it play out in his brain. All of it. Mrs. Lawrence, the little dog and Lizzie, fearful but determined. The rain, the water, creeping in on her. It knocked the air from his lungs and coiled something cold and jagged around his heart. Reaching for her hand had been instinctive and natural. Her hand was cold, her fingers icy—but still a comfort. Holding on to her assured him she was here and safe. The only things to fear now were the memories that kept her trapped in the past.

She squeezed his hand. He squeezed back.

The silence stretched so long that he wondered if she'd decided to stop there. He'd understand. The last thing he wanted to do was push.

When she did start talking again, her voice was softer. "Now the dog had no place to go—I'd get her and we'd leave and everything would be okay." She shrugged. "But a tree limb broke overhead, fell onto the house and crashed through the roof. Somehow, it wedged itself against the pantry door." Her fingers tightened around his. "The wind overhead... It howled. Just howled. I mentioned I have an overdeveloped imagination, before... But this, I'd never imagined something like this." Her fingers ran through Sierra's snow-white fur over and over. "I realized things were...bad. *Bad* bad. We were trapped. The water was coming in, under the door and through the hole in the roof now, too... I didn't know how we'd get out."

The hitch in her breath tore at his heart. She had no idea how brave she was. None. Her fear was real, and, dammit, now he knew why. Being trapped—with the roar of a hurricane outside... Since he couldn't pull her into his lap and hold her close, he cradled her hand in both of his.

She stared at their twined fingers and cleared her throat, her voice a little stronger now. "It was so...dark. Outside. Inside... I couldn't see anything, Hayden. Nothing. That's when my imagination didn't help. I didn't know what was brushing against my feet and legs..." She shuddered. "Silly, I know."

He shook his head. "Understandable." This was one of those times he wished he was better with words.

"Maybe." Her gaze darted his way, then back to their hands. "But Taffy was whining and I had to protect her." She cleared her throat again. "I focused on that—for Mrs. Lawrence. The water kept rising so I climbed the pantry shelves. I thought we'd be okay then. Until the ceiling started collapsing."

His thumb was running across her knuckles. One minute, she'd felt hope—the next defeat and fear all over again. Trapped. In the dark. Alone. He replayed their time together. Each and every twitch and pause, every spatial assessment or full-body stop... Even her reaction to the workshop. The countless times she'd stared out the window at the sky. All of it made sense now. All of it. He hurt for her.

"All I could do was yell. So, I did. Yelled and yelled. But I couldn't get us out... Eventually, I gave up. I made peace with it." Her voice wavered and his hold tightened on hers, offering her a gentle squeeze.

"If you'd given up, you wouldn't be here." He spoke gently, her soft admission revealing so much more. "You didn't give up."

She didn't look at him, but her lips pressed tight for a few minutes before she went on. "Then I heard something. A boat—you know, the little fishing boats with the outboard motors? People, ordinary people, had started searching for survivors." She sucked in a deep breath. "I didn't think I had a voice left but I heard that boat and I screamed with everything I had." She shrugged. "It was only two days—forty-seven hours according to the paramedics… But it seemed…well, a lot longer."

PTSD was the result of enduring or witnessing a traumatic event. This, days of being trapped in a constantly precarious situation with no hope of rescue, more than qualified. He was staring at her openly now. She wasn't just struggling with what had happened, she was struggling with the belief that she'd given up hope—accepted her fate.

"I am sorry, Lizzie. I kept pushing you to talk." He shook his head. "I'm an ass—"

"You are not. You've done…all this. It's just a story now." She looked at him then, really looked at him. "It's okay. I'm okay. Taffy is okay." She frowned. "I mean, I *am* okay—unless this is happening." She glanced out the window, rain streaming across the glass. "Then I act…well, you know. You've seen it."

Yes, he'd seen it. Now he saw it for what it was. "Give yourself some credit. What you've been through? Healing takes time. It's a day-by-day, figure-things-out-as-you-go process. But you're getting stronger." He rubbed her still-cold hand between his. "You hung in there. You fought. You protected Mrs. Lawrence's dog." She turned, but she didn't look at him. Instead, she stared at their hands. "*You* did that. And that's a hell of a lot." He paused. "You hear me?"

Her hazel-green eyes met his. "I hear you."

"Good." He searched her gaze, willing her to believe him. "I'd say you're doing pretty well right now." Thunder cracked overhead, as if emphasizing his point.

A silence stretched between them. Hayden tried his best not to read anything into it. But the longer she looked at him, the harder it was to breathe.

"Because of Sierra," she whispered. "And…you."

It was the last thing he'd expected her to say. The tightness in his chest made it hard for him to say, "I haven't done a thing that any decent person wouldn't have done, Lizzie." He didn't add the rest—that having her here had made him happier than he'd felt in…so long. Or that he hoped the rain kept falling so she'd stay. *She wouldn't stay if it wasn't for the storm—it wouldn't be her choice.* He was a damn fool if he let himself believe otherwise. She'd go and life would go on. "When you and Sierra go home, I'll feel better knowing she's taking care of you." He hadn't meant to say that out loud. He hadn't meant to reach up and brush one long, silky-soft curl from her face or run his thumb along the curve of her cheek.

"You will?" Those beautiful eyes widened, a flare of heat drawing him in.

He nodded, words failing him, his hand still hovering by her cheek. All it took was one look from her, one touch, and he was on fire. So fast. So sure. He didn't try to fight it—he didn't want to. He'd sit here and burn if she kept looking at him that way.

When she leaned into his palm, her eyes fluttering closed, his lungs emptied. Watching her... There was nothing gentle about the tug in his chest. Not this time. If he'd been standing, the force of it would have landed him on his knees. As it was, he explored the soft curve of her cheek she pressed against his work-roughened fingers, which were too rough to touch something so soft. But her hand covered his, held it in place, and there was no fighting her. Touching her felt right. Sitting here, listening, being here with her, was right.

The air between them sparked. The ache was there, stronger than ever, but it was tempered with something infinitely sweeter. "I don't know how this happened," he whispered, his voice husky.

Instead of asking for clarification, she smiled.

His slow exhalation of breath was unsteady. He heard it.

So did she.

He knew what he wanted. Giving in to Lizzie Vega would be all too easy. And, damn, but the sheer force of the current pulling them together was strong. But that didn't mean she wanted this, too. As much as he wanted to believe that she ached for him this way, there was only one way to find out. "Lizzie, I want to kiss—"

Her lips found his. There was nothing restrained about the way her arms tightened around his neck. When he pulled her close, her full-body shudder was answer enough. Her response silenced any and all reservations he had about what was happening. Lizzie was the only person who'd ever stirred a response so potent his normal methodical, cautious and logical analysis before action didn't stand a chance. He was damn near drowning in Lizzie—and he didn't mind a bit.

His hands cradled her face, tilting her head just enough to deepen the kiss. Her lips, so soft, parted. The warmth of her mouth, the brush of her tongue along his, the taste of her...

Charley was the one that put a stop to it. He nosed between them, wiggling and pushing until he'd forced the two of them to return to reality.

Charley was clearly agitated by what was happening. Ears alert, rapid glances between him and Lizzie, a soft whine—the dog was confused. Hayden gave him a solid pat. "It's all good, Charley."

Charley yawned, gave Lizzie another look and sat, staring back and forth between them.

What happened next? He didn't know. But the space didn't ease how he was feeling. The current, more like undertow, still had a firm hold on him. At the same time, he knew things were moving fast. In reality, too fast.

Looking at Lizzie was a mistake. Rosy flushed cheeks. Wide-eyed stare. Lips parted, breath erratic... There was no fear he was in this alone. She wanted him—maybe as much as he wanted her.

She sat back against the kitchen cabinet, breathing hard. Her gaze wandered to his mouth. "You're smiling?" she whispered.

"I am." He shook his head. "Guess Charley thought I needed rescuing."

Lizzie's cheeks went a shade darker as she pushed off the floor. "I don't know about that. But these cinnamon rolls might if we don't finish."

Cinnamon rolls? He didn't give a damn about cinnamon rolls. Not after what had just happened…

She smiled down at him. "What's that look? I can't waste food, Hayden. My grammy would never forgive me."

He didn't miss the way her attention wandered to his mouth. Or the surge of color in her cheeks. She spun away from him but he'd heard the hitch in her breath. He stood and joined her at the kitchen counter. "Can I help?" he offered, standing closer than he needed to.

"If you'd like." She stared up at him. "If there's something else you were wanting to do—"

With one arm, he pulled her against his chest. "I was pretty happy kissing you. Wouldn't mind doing it again," he said, waiting for her to stand on tiptoes for his kiss. When she did, he was smiling. The first kiss was a soft kiss. "Again." This time, his lips clung a little longer. "And again." His voice was hoarse now, his hold on her tightening. "I just want this." He lifted his head. "If that's okay with you?"

* * *

Lizzie was on fire. For all she knew, a tornado could be raging outside and it wouldn't matter. Not with Hayden wrapping her up against him. And his mouth. His kiss… It was dizzying, the effect he had on her. But she welcomed this newly discovered all-consuming hunger for him.

Except the kisses had stopped and he was waiting for her answer. Close enough for his breath to fan across her cheek. Too far for her lips to resume the kissing she was oh so willing to continue.

"Lizzie?" he murmured.

"Yes… This is okay with me." She nodded, slightly breathless.

"After the cinnamon rolls."

What? No. At the moment, she'd be fine scraping the dough into the trash.

"Wouldn't want to upset your grammy." He ran his thumb along her jaw. "And Weston will appreciate it."

Was he serious? Or was he only teasing her about Grammy and Weston. "That's true."

He frowned. So, he was teasing. "Or we could toss it and—"

"No… You're right." With a sigh, she pushed out of his hold, washed her hands in the sink and went back to rolling out the dough. A quick look from the corner of her eye saw he wasn't happy. "Don't blame me, you were the one that played the grandmother and the adorable baby card. These cinnamon rolls are getting made."

His sigh of disappointment almost made her laugh. "They better be incredible."

Now Lizzie was laughing. She had to. Until she noticed that he was staring at her again…his jaw going tight as his gaze focused on her mouth.

He tore his gaze from her and said, "Best cinnamon rolls ever."

"They will be. It's a family recipe. A pinch of this, a pinch of that and butter."

"Pinch?" He was watching her. "We own measuring spoons and cups, if that's easier."

Lizzie paused. "No. I remember once, Grammy was teaching my little cousins—they all call me their aunt—to make biscuits. One of them, Zia, put a measuring cup on the counter, with the rest of the supplies, and Grammy looked downright offended."

Hayden smiled. "She sounds like a character."

"She is. Full of spirit. My mother used to say we were two peas in a pod—she'd never leave me alone with Grammy for too long because she said I was extra hardheaded afterward."

"Does your mother live in Houston, too?"

"Mama died. Cancer." As always, the hole in her heart caused by losing her mother ached. "I was seventeen—about to graduate from high school. I had more than a year to prepare but I don't think you can ever truly prepare for that sort of loss." She shrugged.

"She had always wanted the best for me. She worked three jobs, odd hours, anything to save up to send me to college. She never got the chance to go so I promised her I'd get my degree, have a career, have my name on the door of my own office and make her proud. I hope I've done that."

He nodded. "I'm sure you have."

She sprinkled more flour on the counter. "Losing a parent leaves a hole in your heart, doesn't it?"

"It does. I still miss him every damn day." His nod was curt. "We'd been in town, picking up range cubes for the cattle and swapping bad jokes with the guys that work at the feed store—just like we'd done a hundred times or so. I was still learning to drive so he'd let me drive to town and I was feeling pretty proud of myself." He shook his head. "Dad went from smiling to collapsing in the feed store parking lot."

Lizzie stopped moving, a hard lump in her throat. "You were there?"

He nodded.

"Oh, Hayden…" She didn't know what to say, so she said what was in her heart. "I… That would have been terrifying."

"I didn't know CPR—no one there that day did." His gaze met hers. "The week after the funeral, the city volunteer fire department held a free CPR class in the high school gym. Just about everyone in Granite Falls showed up to learn. That's something Dad would have loved, bringing people together like that. It would have meant the world to him."

"Sounds like he was loved." She suspected Hayden was a lot like his father. A good man—and well loved.

"He was. If you knew him, you respected him." He nodded. "The sort of man I want Weston to grow into."

She had to smile then. "He will. He has you for his daddy." It was hard to tear her gaze from his. Standing here, talking, just being next to him, soothed an ache someplace deep inside. It wasn't the first time she'd struggled to understand the whirlpool of emotions he stirred. But, now, it felt like things had changed.

"That's next. Sprinkle it all over." She nodded at the bowl with the cinnamon, sugar and butter crumble. "The more, the gooier."

He cocked an eyebrow. "Is gooier better for a toddler?"

"Gooier is better for everyone. But let's make sure it's right." She dipped her finger into the bowl.

Hayden watched as she sucked the cinnamon sugar from her finger, his eyes narrowing and his jaw clenched tight.

If she'd been weak-kneed and aching before…the way he was looking at her now? She pushed the bowl his way and washed her hands in the sink until her heart rate had slowed.

Yes, this attraction was powerful and alive but, for her, there was more to it. When she looked at him, her body wasn't the only thing that seemed to perk up and take notice—her heart did, too. There was no way, no way, her heart could get involved.

Hayden and her didn't make sense. They were from different worlds. Her world was far from here. She had a job she loved. A job she'd given up dates, holidays and vacations for. A job that gave her the status and respect her mother had wanted for her.

Add that to her failed relationship attempts and her PTSD from the hurricane... She wasn't exactly a catch for someone like Hayden Mitchell.

Not that there was any indication that he was anything but attracted to her. *Way to get way, way ahead of yourself, Lizzie.*

But she remembered the look on his face as he'd murmured, *I don't know how this happened*, and her resolve was shaken. What if he hadn't just been talking about the pull between them? What if, like her, he felt something more? *Because falling in love with someone in, what, two days' time isn't all that unusual.* Love? Where had that come from? She wasn't falling in love with Hayden. No way. Whatever she was feeling, it was not love.

"Good?" he asked, standing aside—waiting for her approval.

"Looks great." She nodded, instantly distracted by his smile. And the thump of her heart because of that smile. *Stop it.* This was all circumstantial. The weather. The isolation. The attraction. *Temporary.* She needed to remember that.

"I'll get started on cleanup," Hayden offered, moving around her to the sink full of dishes and the dishwasher beside that.

In two days, I'll leave and it will be like none of this ever happened. She glanced his way, her breath catching at the sight of him bending forward. The rear view of Hayden Mitchell was almost as good as the front. Definitely not the sort of thing she'd forget. *Who am I kidding?* There was no forgetting Hayden or Weston—or her time here. Even if she could, why would she want to?

She rolled up the dough, pulled out a large knife and started cutting individual cinnamon rolls and placing them in the two lined baking pans.

She'd just finished putting the trays in the refrigerator when the whir of cicadas and crickets was surprisingly loud in the kitchen. A look around the room said why.

"Charley." Hayden sighed, crossing the great room to the wide-open back door. "Never should have taught him that trick." He pushed the door closed, returning the nature sounds to a more muted level, and turned the lock.

Charley hung his head, every bit the remorseful dog.

"He's not mad at you, Charley," she cooed, catching sight of Hayden's eye roll. "Nope, Hayden is grumpy with himself for not locking the door."

Charley wagged his tail.

She laughed, looking up to find Hayden watching her. The spark in his gaze ignited a fire deep in the pit of her belly. Instant and molten and craving...Hayden.

She didn't remember moving but she must have—since she was in his arms, against his chest, staring up at his face and those warm eyes.

He smiled, tilting her chin up. But he didn't kiss her, not right away. Instead, he seemed to be studying her. He reached back to brush her hair from her shoulders. But he still didn't kiss her. And she really, really wanted him to kiss her.

"Are you going to kiss me?" She swallowed.

"I am." He was smiling, his hands steady on her waist. He was going to kiss her. He was. He'd done it twice now and both times he'd looked just like this before he'd bent forward and pressed his mouth to hers. She waited, her fingers pleating the front of his cotton shirt, holding her breath.

"Now would be good." She smiled at him, her pulse picking up as he closed the distance between them.

"Like this?" he asked.

"Close," she whispered, her smile growing as he pulled her against him. "Almost there." Her arms slid around his neck and, on tiptoe, she kissed until he growled low in his throat and pulled her against him. That sound made every nerve tingle.

His lips lifted from hers, trailing across her cheek to her temple, then her ear, and she was gasping for air. The featherlight brush of his lips on her neck rocked her to her toes. His breath was hot against the sensitive skin behind her ear. She leaned into him. His lips caressed the curve of her ear before drawing her earlobe into his mouth and sending a shudder down her spine. She didn't recognize the sound she made—didn't realize she'd made it—until he'd pulled back to look at her. Whatever he saw gave him permission to continue his exploration of her neck and ear. Every kiss and suck and nibble had her arching into him.

His hands moved, too. Sliding through her hair, stroking the curve of her neck, pressing flat at the base of her spine, or running his fingertips slowly up her spine. And she welcomed it, welcomed him.

When his lips brushed her cheek, she turned into him. Her mouth found his and the very tip of her tongue traced the inside of his lower lip. His hands slid up to cradle her face, holding her, while the kiss went on and on.

It wasn't enough. Not anymore. The more he kissed her, the more she wanted.

His hand slid beneath her shirt, his fingers trailing along her belly. When the heat of his open palm pressed against her side, skin to skin, she trembled.

Nothing felt this good. Nothing. Only Hayden. His touch. His kiss.

"Lizzie." Her name had never sounded so sweet. One word, broken and raw and asking for what they both wanted. "I'm asking for more than a kiss this time."

"Ask." She dared to meet his gaze, to dive into the blazing hunger in those fathomless brown eyes. "The answer is yes."

His gaze swept over her face before he stepped back, took her hand in his and led her to his room. As soon as the door shut, she was aching with need and desire. Hayden's gaze, unflinchingly admiring, emboldened her enough to take what she wanted. Him.

Her hands tugged the hem of his shirt. He pulled it up and over his head, dropping it on the floor at their feet. That chest... For the second time, she was blindsided by the true rugged beauty of his form. Because, really, she'd never seen anyone like him—not in real life. And she'd certainly never, ever touched a man like this.

With a single step forward, there was no space or air that Hayden didn't occupy. And—*oh my*—his skin beneath her hand was wholly distracting. She shrugged out of the oversize shirt. Braless, she pulled the string tie of her pants and removed any barrier between them. The shock of skin-to-skin contact had her moaning.

Hayden's shudder-inducing sound had her melting as they fell together onto the bed. His touch grew more feverish, his lips hungrier, but there was also an aching tenderness when their gazes met—stirring more than her body.

When all clothing disappeared, she wasn't certain. He was doing far too good a job at occupying her senses to care about anything beyond him. In that moment, she suspected another hurricane could hit and she wouldn't flinch—not if he continued to explore and nuzzle the curve of her breast. Hands and mouth, he rained affection down on her until she couldn't take it anymore.

Thankfully, he was on the same page.

With a long, searing kiss, his lips parted hers—as her legs parted for him. Her fingers grasped at his well-muscled back, arching up to meet him as he slid deep into her body. She was fighting to breathe, the slow rhythm he set the sweetest torture. His mouth lifted from hers, the uneven rasp of his breath stoking a fire she was certain couldn't burn any hotter.

Oh, how happy she was to be wrong.

Every touch, every thrust, every hitch of breath drew her pleasure higher. His hands slid along her sides, clasping her hips, and holding her to him. Before long, there was nothing slow about the way their bodies came together. She held on, her gaze locking with his. The passion on his face and hunger in his eyes was raw—and potent. There was no stopping the rising tide of pleasure he stirred. On and on until she was strung tight, on the edge, so close... And then she was caught up in a storm of sensation. Powerful. Consuming. Running along every nerve ending and shattering whatever remaining control she had. For those few seconds, she was lost in Hayden and the way he made her feel. He fell apart soon after. The flare of his nostrils, the tensing of his back beneath her hands and sudden clenching of his jaw giving way to a low, rough groan. He rolled to her side and rested his hand on her stomach.

It took a long time for her heart to slow—longer for her breathing to even out and return to normal. But then she turned to find Hayden watching her, heavy-lidded and grinning. His fingertips stroked a lazy trail from her stomach all the way to her temple, brushing her hair back.

"Hi," she whispered, rolling onto her side to face him.

"Hi, yourself." His gaze locked with hers.

Strange that she was nervous *now*. Not when she'd been moaning beneath him, no. But lying here, staring at each other, was giving her a serious case of... butterflies. His hand caressed the side of her face, drawing attention to the contours of his arm. Some arm. Attached to that chest. The chest she was now staring at.

"What are you thinking?" He propped himself up on an elbow and stared down at her, drawing lazy circles on her bare stomach with his other hand.

His body. Here he was, leaning over her, all muscles and sheer…*maleness*. Naked and in bed, with the sheets tangled around them and her breathing barely returned to normal. All she could think about was him. What he did to her. How he made her feel. Not just her body, her heart, too.

Because… Her heart *was* involved.

Hayden was waiting for her answer, studying her face.

She couldn't tell him what she was thinking *now*. Something told her he'd freak out if she said she was developing an emotional connection with him. *She* was freaking out. She hadn't intended to blurt out, "That was… Wow." *Wow? Really?* "Lovely. Incredible. I'm stopping now."

His gaze swept over her face, intent. "I agree with the *wow*." His smile was slow, but powerful.

The smile. The stare. The chest. Those lips… He demanded her full attention. All of him. What was it about Hayden Mitchell that made her heart full and her brain malfunction? Why did she keep thinking about her heart where Hayden was involved? Better not to overanalyze things. Not tonight, anyway.

His fingers brushed along her temple, the corner of his mouth cocking up before he leaned forward to press a kiss against her forehead. Right before he kissed her, before she was lost in Hayden and all the wonderful sensations he caused, he smiled at her. And that smile…

And just like that she knew. It was too late. How could she guard her heart when it already belonged to him?

Chapter Thirteen

It was two in the morning and they were raiding the kitchen. Considering the way they'd worked up their appetite, Hayden had no complaints. But a quick search revealed only one option. A fresh-baked cinnamon roll. Or two. Now the kitchen was scented with cinnamon and sugar. Lizzie had baked five baking sheets full of rolls, then whipped up some honey-sweet glaze he'd happily licked from each of Lizzie's fingertips.

As much as he'd like to deny it, the intimacy they'd established in his bedroom was wavering. Lizzie seemed skittish now, almost as if she was trying to put space between them. Was it because what they'd shared in his bed was a one-off sort of thing for her? He didn't believe that. So it must be that she was afraid to acknowledge all the things they were both trying to dance around. Like what, exactly, was happening between them. But, if she wasn't ready to talk about it, he wasn't going to push. Tonight had been about as perfect a night as he'd ever had and he didn't want it to end. For now, he'd leave it alone and eat cinnamon rolls until his stomach hurt.

"I thought we made more than this." She glanced at the single cinnamon roll on the plate.

"We did. I ate them." He patted his stomach and smiled.

Her eyes widened. "You did? I don't know whether to be impressed or concerned."

He smiled.

She paused then, her gaze lifting from his mouth to meet his gaze. "Has anyone ever told you that you have a...nice smile?"

"I don't think so." But he liked hearing her say it. He hooked his arm around her waist. "Anyone ever told you you're beautiful?" He liked it when her cheeks flushed. "And you're a hell of a baker."

"Another backup option." She shrugged. "Nanny or baker."

Which brought him around to their earlier conversation. "If you're not sure about returning to the university, I'm sure there are other places that would want you."

"Like the new high school here in Granite Falls?" she asked, her hazel eyes falling from his.

So she hadn't missed his mother's less-than-subtle suggestion. Of course, she hadn't. She was a smart woman. And, in case there had been any doubt, his mother had circled the job opening in bright yellow highlighter. "If that's what you wanted, why not?"

"I'm not sure what I want anymore." She glanced up at him, then returned to staring at her hands resting against his chest.

That wasn't a no. Why the hell did that have to make him so happy? It shouldn't. Not in the least. Until now, he'd made a concerted effort not to think about what happened once he dropped her off at her car. But now... Well, he more than liked the idea of her staying here. "That's okay."

"Is it?" she asked, looking up at him. "I've always known what I needed to do next. I'm definitely goal-oriented." She shrugged, stepping out of his hold to busy herself in the kitchen. "I love my job. I've worked hard for it." But her smile didn't reach her eyes.

In the short time she'd been here, he'd started to realize her process. If something was weighing on her, she had to physically occupy herself. He had yet to determine if it was a distraction mechanism or a way for her to work through things. Considering the ferocity with which she was wiping down the counter she'd already cleaned, he figured something was weighing on her.

She shrugged. "I want to be Dr. Elizabeth Vega, art professor. That's who I am. I wanted to make my mother proud."

It wasn't the first time she'd said that. Honoring her mother was important to Lizzie—hell, it might be the key motivating factor in every facet of Lizzie's life. But, deep down, he suspected what Lizzie's mother truly wanted was for her only daughter to be happy. At the end of the day, that's what any parent wanted. "She wanted you to be a professor?"

"She wanted me to make something of myself. She said the more initials after my name, the better." Lizzie stared around the spotless kitchen. "She worked so hard—for *me*. I guess, because she never got a degree, becoming a professor was a way to honor her."

"You're a good daughter, Lizzie. She would be proud." He paused, then asked, "What about what you want?"

"I am doing what I want." She shot him a look. "I mean, I think I am… No, I *know* I am. And now… If I quit, the storm wins. It's driven me off. Stolen my career. If I stay…" She broke off, shrugging.

"The storm wins?" How he wanted to hold her then. "Lizzie, forget about the damn storm for a minute—"

"You think I haven't tried that?" she bit back, the tilt of her head defiant. "I wish it was that easy."

"I didn't mean that." He sighed, running his hand over the top of his head. "I mean, you can't base your decisions on what happened. Don't let the past affect your future. If you could choose to be anything, anywhere, what would it be?"

She was staring at him but her expression was shuttered. He had no idea what she was thinking—and he hated it. The longer she stared at him, the more he regretted asking the question. Hell, he regretted this whole damn conversation.

She cleared her throat. "Hayden, I've been working toward this for so long, it was almost like it was the *only* option." She swallowed. "Now, well, I'm supposed to start over? I don't know how I would do that. Where I would go? The Houston Art Institute or the California Art Conservatory…or the Granite Falls High School Art Department?" She shrugged. "It's not that easy… It's my life we're talking about."

He nodded, determined to keep his mouth shut in the hopes she'd talk to him. While she never said it outright, he was beginning to believe she didn't have a sounding board.

"When I'm on campus, I'm Dr. Elizabeth Vega." She ran a hand over her borrowed T-shirt. "There are so few tenured spots anymore, there's no room for anything else. If I want to keep my spot, I have to put in the work. So I do. I have to. Even if I'm tired.

It's not just my mother. It's my grammy, too. She was the one who fostered my love of art. It was something we did together—and it worried my mother." She shrugged. "Momma wanted me to support myself. Grammy wanted me to express myself. My job does both—makes them both happy. Do you understand?" Once he nodded, she went on, "And I do love teaching. I do. So much that I filled in at the senior center for Mrs. Lawrence and her friends. Considering how bossy and opinionated my students were, I'd have to love what I was doing. But, for all their prickly exterior, they're all so dear. So like Grammy, especially Mrs. Lawrence."

Which shed new light on her ordeal in the closet. It was clear Lizzie would do anything for her family—or the people she considered family.

Her smile was brilliant, her hands moving and her features animated. "I worked with the programs director to provide crafts that stimulated arthritic joints and required attention to fine motor skills—but they didn't know they were doing something therapeutic. To them, it was art time." She rolled her eyes, still smiling. "After that, my senior class was getting me to volunteer for camps and classes teaching their grandchildren. That was just as fun, in a different way." Her gaze fell from his. "But *fun* doesn't pay the bills or put food on the table or...or honor the memory of the woman who worked so hard to give me the world."

"You think your mother would be disappointed in those things? You, making people happy?" he asked. "Filling a hole in a child's development or providing physical therapy to a senior?"

"When you put it that way, it sounds almost noble but—"

"There is nothing wrong with being happy, Lizzie." He smiled. "You were all animated and excited just talking about it. Maybe, in your heart, you already know what you want to do."

She swallowed, her eyes meeting his. "But wanting something doesn't mean it's the right thing, Hayden—even if it makes you happy. You know that just as much as I do."

Maybe it was the way her gaze fell from his or the way her voice trailed off but he wasn't sure she was just talking about her career anymore. But that didn't stop him from wanting to argue with her. He didn't stop to question why.

He leaned back against the kitchen counter, doing his best to act unaffected. "A couple of years ago, I'd agree. But now, after everything life has thrown my way, I think being happy should be a priority. Might not always be practical. Might not always be easy. But worthwhile? Definitely." He definitely wasn't talking about her career anymore. It made no sense but she made him happy. In a short snippet of time, she'd filled an emptiness he hadn't acknowledged.

Now that he had…well, there was no going back. If only he knew how to move forward.

"You're happy, then?" she asked, almost a whisper. "As is?"

"I'm working on it." It was an honest answer. Even standing on opposite sides of the kitchen was too much space between them. Was it him? Or did she feel the pull between them? He pushed off the edge of the countertop, drew in a deep breath and closed the space between them. The crackle and spark practically arced between them, electrifying the air. "I mean, we've got cinnamon rolls. That's a step in the right direction." His voice was surprisingly rough.

"That's true." She nodded, her voice softening as she stared up at him. "Is there anything that can top one of those, fresh for breakfast, on the happiness scale? Pretty sure they are way up there."

Since he'd reached the point of no return, there was no reason to hold back. He swallowed and threw caution to the wind. "I can think of something that tops them." His fingers traced the curve of her jaw. "If I didn't prove that the first time, I'm happy to try again." He saw her hesitant smile, the way she blew out a slow breath—and then she was in his arms and the rest of the world melted away.

Lizzie lay in her bed, a smile on her face. Beside her, Hayden snored softly, one arm draped across her stomach. She didn't know what sort of dream this was—it had to be a dream—but she so didn't want to wake up. As soon as the sun was up, the real world would return. Honestly, she didn't know what that looked like anymore.

For the moment, she was content.

Sleeping Hayden was just as gorgeous as Hayden awake. So far, she had yet to see Hayden in anything other than gorgeous mode. Not that she was complaining. Not in the least. After last night… Well, she had no complaints.

She was contemplating her morning greeting options when his eyes opened. A few heavy-lidded blinks and he was giving her a sleepy smile.

"Good morning," he murmured.

After a moment's hesitation, she rolled onto her side to face him. "Good morning."

He smoothed the mess of curls from her cheek, letting one long curl slide between his fingers. "Sleep okay?"

She nodded. "You?"

He smothered a yawn with the back of his hand. "Like a baby." He sighed. "Speaking of… What time is it?"

"Five thirty—give or take a minute." The house was quiet, but not for much longer.

His soft groan ended with a frown.

"Too late? Or too early?" she asked.

"I told Bobby I'd ride out with him early. He's worried about the fencing along the creek bed." He ran a hand over his face, his gaze sweeping over her face. "I hadn't planned on sleeping in."

"This is sleeping in?" She smiled.

"Not normally, no." He leaned forward, pressing a soft kiss to her lips. "But I was sort of hoping we had more time."

"You were?" she whispered, relieved.

"Weston should sleep until I'm back." He nodded, his lips soft against her ear. He pulled back, frowning slightly. "You going to be okay?"

"Why wouldn't I be?" she asked, distracted by the feel of his fingers trailing down her spine. If he kept this up, she was going to be more than okay...

He stopped the gentle stroking along her back and propped himself over her, that crooked grin on his face. "You don't hear that?"

She blinked, disappointed by the sudden lack of contact. "What?"

He pointed up, his smile growing.

It was raining. Hard.

"Oh." She frowned, beyond surprised. When had that started? How had she not heard it? "Huh."

"I think I'm going to have to take credit for this." One brow arched, he nodded. He was totally hamming it up.

"Yes, you cured me." It was so hard not to laugh at the expression he was wearing. "Or I'm exhausted."

"Either way, it works." He ran his nose along her neck. "But I was thinking we might need to do this a few more times. Really test the theory." The brush of warm breath was followed by a featherlight kiss at the base of her throat.

"You…" She swallowed. "You think pretty highly of yourself." But it took effort to get the words out— since he was still proving his point.

With a sigh, he stopped and looked down at her. "I admit, it feels pretty good."

All she could do was stare back at him. He was… Well, it was some view. Not to mention that he had thoroughly distracted her from the rain.

With another sigh, he sat up. "You make it hard to get out of bed."

"I didn't do a thing," she argued, propping herself on the pillows. "You were the one doing…all the things."

He chuckled. "All the things, huh?"

"Well, maybe not *all* the things. But, you know, things would have progressed if you didn't have fences to fix."

"Just remember you're stuck here at least one more night so…" He shrugged. "I'm thinking *all* the things will be done."

There was no holding back her smile now.

"Glad to see you're on board." He pressed another kiss to her forehead and slid from the bed.

If she thought the earlier view was impressive, the rear view of fully naked Hayden was doubly so. Every inch of him was like carved marble, smooth yet chiseled to perfection. In a very warm, human way, of course. "How is it possible for you to look like that?" Yes—the words came out of her mouth. Not a thought kept to herself. Actually spoken.

He turned, effectively knocking the air from her lungs with yet another mind-blowing display of pure masculine perfection. "Look like what? Bad? Good? I'm not sure."

She covered her face with both hands and sank down into the pillows. "Good. Very good," she squeaked, peeking through her fingers to fully appreciate all the Hayden on display.

"Oh, well, okay, then." He was smiling, tugging on his jeans and sliding his skintight white undershirt over his head. When his gaze met hers, he seemed to be considering his words carefully. Just when she thought he was finally going to say whatever he was thinking, he paused. She was on pins and needles by the time he finally said, "You're stronger than you give yourself credit for, Lizzie. Keep thinking good things until I get back." His gaze held hers, to emphasize the impact of his words.

How could words fill her with such happiness? Possibly—likely—because his opinion was important… Her heart thumped against her rib cage, hard. The realization was all the more sobering when she realized he was dressed and ready to leave. Into the brewing storm. "Is it safe?" But the words were soft and garbled. She cleared her throat and tried again. "You'll be careful?" She pulled her knees to her chest and wrapped her arms around them.

"Always." He nodded, the reluctance on his face warming her through. He opened the door and Sierra and Charley trotted in. "You two will watch over things until I get back?"

Sierra's tail wagged.

"Good," he said, giving Lizzie a parting glance. And then he was gone. She flopped back on the bed and stared up at the rough-hewn beams overhead. The bed seemed extra big now that she was alone in it. She rolled over, burying her face in the pillow next to her. It smelled like Hayden. Sadly, it couldn't fill the void left by his arms and lips and the beat of his heart beneath her ear...

A distant rumble caught her ear and she sat up, her gaze shifting to the large window. There was no sign of sunlight. And, from the slight rattle of the glass in the pane, Bobby's storm predictions were coming true.

Sierra put one paw on the edge of the bed. Charley cocked his head to one side, then turned and trotted out of the bedroom.

"Guess he has plans." Lizzie nodded, running her hand along the Sierra's broad head. "I hear it now." She waited for the terror to wind itself around her heart. "You can come up here, you know." She patted the bed. "If you want."

Sierra cocked her head to one side, glancing between her and the bed.

Lizzie patted the bed again. "It's just me and you, Sierra. Two single, carefree ladies out to conquer the world." Single, carefree and pathetic sounding. It was a choice she'd made—to put her career first. And now… Well, she'd been perfectly content as a strong, independent woman. She would be again. Wouldn't she?

Sierra jumped up onto the bed beside her and lay down, pressed against her thigh. Would Sierra be happy with just her? After all, Lizzie's life was pretty boring. Well, when she wasn't having a panic attack over the weather, that is. The dog rested her head on Lizzie's calf and sighed loudly.

"All that?" Lizzie laughed.

Sierra yawned.

"I'm glad you're not concerned." She proceeded to give Sierra a full-body rubdown—focusing 100 percent on the dog. The rain grew steadier now; she could hear it. But fear-induced paralysis had yet to kick in. Yes, her heart was a little fast. And yes, she felt…tense. So far, it was bearable. Not so much for her, though. For Hayden—who was out in the thick of it. She was holding it together pretty well. "So far, so good."

Sierra snored in answer.

The rain grew heavier, a distant rumble promising thunder—possibly lightning. *I'm okay.* Now was the perfect time to test herself. She wasn't alone. She had Sierra. If there was reason to be alarmed, she'd let Lizzie know.

And, if things got really bad, Hayden would come running... *Wait.* She dissected that out-of-nowhere assertion several times over. In the end, she reached the same conclusion. She knew it, with absolute certainty, that Hayden *would* be there—if she needed him. Her heart was thumping heavily again. "How do I feel about that?" she asked Sierra.

Other than a sleep-twitch, Sierra didn't respond.

"We're leaving, you know," she whispered. Of course, they were leaving. It had been...days. Good days, some of the best really. Days full of Weston and Hayden, shared meals, story time, cooking and cleaning and being together. Almost like a family.

But this isn't my family. She shoved aside the sudden ache in her chest.

As a goal-driven person, she needed a new one. Initially, she'd come with one goal in mind. A dog. Now Sierra was snoring beside her on the bed. Goal met.

What now? She and Hayden had sort of skirted the issue—before she'd fallen into bed with him. *No, don't get distracted. Think. Goals.*

Jobs. She had one. One she'd based every decision on. It didn't make her unhappy. Hayden meant well, but how could she give up everything she'd worked for...for what? It's not like she and Hayden had ever mentioned a future. Did she want to risk her career after a couple of days? Wonderful days, certainly. But not real? Surely? None of this would last. She and Hayden… Well, there was no she and Hayden. Not really.

If she considered changing jobs, it would be for the right reasons. What sort of growth potential? Income? Fulfillment? And nothing, absolutely nothing, to do with Hayden.

Besides, it wasn't like Hayden had asked her to stay.

"What am I doing?" she asked, pushing off the bed and heading down the hall to her room and into the guest bathroom. She used the toothbrush Hayden had located that first night, pulled her hair into a knot and stuck her tongue out at herself. "You've worked too hard to start basing your future on some…some man." Not just *some* man. Hayden. Hayden who… who… Where to start? She'd never met anyone like him—never connected so quickly. She *had* slept with him. For her, that was a big deal. Sex had never been a casual thing. And, since she was falling in love with him, there had been a rightness to it—

"No." *Falling in love?* She shook her head. "I am not." No, she wasn't falling in love with Hayden Mitchell. She was already in love with him. "Oh, no. No, no, no," she groaned, more loudly than she'd intended. "Enough of this." She turned to find Sierra sitting up, watching her. "Breakfast?" Anything to get her out of her head until she was thinking more clearly.

She headed for the kitchen, Sierra at her side.

Jan was in the kitchen, making coffee. "Good morning. Hope we didn't wake you."

"No. I didn't realize you were up," Lizzie confessed, hoping Jan Mitchell hadn't caught sight of her returning to her bedroom.

Weston, who was sitting on the floor amid a pile of blocks, clapped his hands. "Hi."

"Good morning, handsome." She waved as she made her way to him and sat on the play mat across from him.

Weston reached forward to pat her leg. "Hi."

Lizzie tapped his little nose. "Hi to you too, you adorable little guy."

Weston squealed, then handed her a block.

"He's so chipper in the morning, it gets the day started off right—even before coffee." Jan chuckled. "Should be ready soon, though."

"Thank you," Lizzie said, stacking the blocks. "How are you feeling?"

"Much better." Jan smiled. "I guess it just had to run its course."

"Stomach bugs are the worst." She laughed as Weston knocked down their block tower. "Can I make breakfast for you? Both of you?"

"I hate for you to—"

"I really like to cook," she interrupted. "Hayden

and I made a pan full of cinnamon rolls from a family recipe. They're delicious." Hopefully, the extralong look Jan Mitchell was giving her was all in her imagination.

"I dreamed about cinnamon rolls." Jan chuckled. "I guess I must have smelled them while I was sleeping." She pulled open the refrigerator. "Looks like you two made enough for an army."

"I guess we got a little carried away." And not just with the cinnamon rolls. Her cheeks were instantly warm.

"Hayden rode out this morning. Bobby called—worried about the creek washing out one of the fences. And, with the rain starting up again, they need to reinforce things before it gets too bad." Jan stopped in front of the back door to peer out into the gloomy sky. "I can't complain. We've needed rain for some time now."

He will be fine. When he got back, he'd be hungry. Hopefully, he'd still be okay with cinnamon rolls. Considering he'd eaten four, he might want something else. "How about some eggs, too? Maybe some bacon." Just in case... She'd make plenty of food for his return.

"Sounds perfect." Thunder cracked overhead, causing them all to pause. "Guess this will delay your departure a little," Jan said, pouring them each a cup of coffee. "Hope that won't cause any problems with work... Or whoever is waiting for you at home."

Her gaze slid to the window. The storm didn't show any signs of letting up. "No. But I am sorry for any inconvenience my staying might cause." It wasn't that the storm didn't bother her—it did. But the longer it stormed, the longer she could stay with Hayden.

"It's no trouble at all." Jan smiled, patting her arm. "My boys both seem pretty content to keep you around. You stay—as long as you like, Lizzie. You hear me? Rain or shine."

"Thank you." Lizzie nodded. If someone had told her she'd want to be stranded longer, she would have laughed. But that was before… Now? Even with the thunder and rain, somehow she was smiling ear to ear. "I'll get breakfast started."

Chapter Fourteen

Hayden wiped at the back of his neck. The rain had lightened up, a mere trickle now, but the earlier showers had soaked him to the bone. As a result of the last three days' rainfall, the creek had widened some, straining the sheep and goat netting stretched across the waterway. It wasn't the constant current of rushing water that snapped the wire. It had been the accumulation of fallen tree limbs and debris that brought the section down. He and Bobby worked in tandem to get the last of the new wire strung tightly into place.

Luckily, the herd had gathered on high ground— far from the creek. While they were completing the fence repair, he'd asked ranch hands Crockett and Jeb to drive the cattle back to the ranch and into a pasture with more coverage.

"Good?" Bobby asked, waiting for Hayden's nod before he let go of the thick wire.

They stepped back, making sure the wire wasn't too tight, before using the pliers to twine the string into place.

"Should have done this yesterday," Hayden said, shaking his head. "You were right." It had been his call to wait.

"I'd have made up excuses myself if I had something as pretty as you do waiting at home." Bobby chuckled. "Guess you can thank the rain for keeping her here, eh?"

He'd be lying if he argued with Bobby. The decision to wait on repairs had been so he could spend more time with Lizzie. Even soaked through, he didn't regret his decision.

"She staying? Once the rain lets up, I mean?" Bobby asked. "Your doctor lady?"

His? He was doing his best to take things a day at a time but... His damn-fool mind had spent one too many hours pondering that very scenario. Lizzie. Staying... But at the end of the day, he always came back to the same conclusion. Once the roads opened, Lizzie would leave. Besides, Lizzie had to learn to stand on her own two feet again. If she didn't, she'd never trust herself enough to decide what she really wanted—what was best for her. Asking her to stay wasn't fair. Not that he was happy about her going. "Just until the roads clear." He bit the words out.

"Huh." Bobby shrugged. "Well, all right, then."

Snapping at Bobby didn't make any sense. The man hadn't done a thing wrong.

"I got the feeling you liked this woman. You like having her around." Bobby started packing up the extra wire into the bed of the mud-covered four-wheel-drive ranch truck.

"You got all that from one meeting?" Hayden asked, shaking his head. He picked up the wire puller, swung it onto his shoulder and carried it around to the rear of the truck.

"Nope." Bobby tipped his hat back. "She was nice and all. And pretty to boot. It was more how you were acting. All squirrelly. On edge. Making a point of not looking at her. Hard not to notice." He shook his head. "And… Well, hell, we didn't do this yesterday, now, did we? I've never, in all the years I've known you, seen *you* put off something that needed to be done. You're up at dawn and winding down at dark—always looking for something to do." Hands on hips, he gave Hayden a once-over. "Since you've been checking your watch or staring up at the sky all morning, I'm thinking you're impatient to get back to something… or someone."

Hayden slid the wire puller into the truck bed

and closed the tailgate. "That's a lot of speculation, Bobby."

"Is it, now?" Bobby chuckled. "Maybe it is. Maybe I'm just paying attention. I'm not pointing nothing out to get you riled. You woo that little lady. Get her to stay. Find yourself a sliver of happiness. Make life less about getting by and more about really living."

Bobby was only ten years or so older than him, but that didn't stop him from spouting off bits of wisdom now and then. Mostly, it had to do with ranching. Come to think of it, he couldn't remember a time Bobby had ever mentioned anything personal. He'd never offered up advice about Karla—and he'd met her on more than one occasion. "That was a mouthful," Hayden said, but he was smiling now.

"It was. Tuckered me out saying it all, too." Bobby shook his head. "Don't mean you shouldn't think what I said over, though, you hear me?"

"I hear you." Hayden nodded, the roar of distant thunder snagging his attention. No need to tell Bobby just how much Lizzie had been weighing on his mind.

"Least we won't be worrying about pumping in water," Bobby said, staring up at the sky and shaking out his coat, revealing a glimpse of red-and-white-striped suspenders beneath. "All this wet should fill up the aquifer and then some."

Hayden agreed. Granite Falls was located over a

massive underground aquifer that supplied water for most of this region of the Hill Country. With each spring seeming dryer and dryer, the last few years had seen more than their fair share of water rationing. Lucky for them, the ranch had its own well on the property—but the rain would help all around.

The louder the thunder grew, the faster Hayden worked. Up until now, the rain had been the worst of it. But, from the rolling black clouds and flashes of lightning, he suspected things were about to get worse. Even though Lizzie had Sierra, his mother and Weston to keep her company, he couldn't shake the need to be there, too.

As they were driving along the deeply rutted path leading through the far pasture and around to the barns, Bobby asked, "You know my Opal?"

"I do." He thought Bobby's wife was a hoot.

"You know she was the one that asked me out?" He shook his head. "Most headstrong woman I've ever met. She kept at me and kept at me until I had no choice but to go. Once I did that, there was no going back." He chuckled. "She was bossy and temperamental and full of opinions. I knew it'd never be easy, she'd see to that. But I knew, without her, life wouldn't have the same color."

Hayden stared out the front windshield, kicking in the four-wheel drive when the tires started throwing up mud and the truck started sliding.

"All I'm asking is, does this Dr. Vega make things

more colorful?" he asked. "You don't have to answer, but you know what I'm getting at."

"I know what you're getting at, Bobby." Hayden chuckled.

"I wasn't trying to be secret-like about it," Bobby snapped. "As Opal would say, time is a wasting."

Hayden shot him a look. "You were saying *Opal* is bossy?"

Bobby scowled. "Where do you think I get it from?"

"You know you could be talking about yourself, don't you?" That had him laughing. "Maybe she's picked up a thing or two from you, ever think of that?"

Bobby grinned. "Might. A time or two."

It had been an interesting way of putting things, though. Adding color? Considering Lizzie's artistic nature and, weather allowing, bright spirit, he'd say *colorful* was a damn near perfect description of the woman.

"Would she say the same about you?" Hayden asked. "Adding color?"

Bobby snorted. "I doubt it. Unless we're talking about all about the gray hair she says I've given her. I'm not sure that counts."

Hayden laughed again, the truck bouncing when it hit a water-filled pothole in the dirt road. That did sound like something Opal would say. For all their teasing, the two of them had a solid marriage.

Just like his mother and father had. They'd provided him and his brothers with a strong appreciation for the work that it took to keep a marriage alive, their friendship unwavering. He and Karla had never mastered that. Then again, the two of them hadn't had much in common—outside of the military.

What do I have in common with Lizzie? Considering the amount of time he'd spent thinking about the woman, it was a valid question. There had to be something beyond overwhelming attraction to keep a couple together. That part they had down.

She was an artist.

He was a soldier-turned-rancher or—how had she put it? A rancher who's also a soldier and dog-human matchmaker. He smiled, shaking his head.

Attraction aside, there was some common ground between them.

They'd both lost parents.

They both worked hard, came from large families and wanted a family of their own.

Now that he knew her a little better, he knew she was strong. She'd been through hell but she wasn't giving up. She'd come here for help—for Sierra. And she'd come alone. But no one had come with her because she probably hadn't asked anyone. So, they had that in common, too. Strength and stubbornness. Or, as John liked to say, pigheadedness.

But she was also gentle and kind. His boy already loved her, all giggles and smiles when he saw her.

She'd thought to take care of his mother, a perfect stranger.

And her smile…

Well, he loved her smile. Not just her smile. If he'd been looking for all the reasons they couldn't be together, it wasn't working. It was only confirming something he knew, something he'd done his best to avoid. Lizzie was… Well, she'd found a place in his heart. He was entering dangerous territory. He drove into the yard, pulling around the back of the barn for cover.

"How did you know?" Hayden asked. "With Opal, I mean. How did you know she was the one?"

"Easy." He shrugged. "I tried to imagine her with someone else." He glanced Hayden's way, wearing a fierce expression. "I couldn't let anyone else have her. After that—well, I'd never been so certain of anything in my life."

Hayden pulled under the overhang of the barn and turned off the engine.

"What about you?" Bobby asked. "You fine with the pretty doctor going off with some other fella?"

The answer was there, hard and heavy against his chest. Hayden sighed, glaring at the older man. "Nope."

Bobby started laughing then. "Didn't think so."

Lightning struck close to the barn, jolting them both around to look out the rear window. The earth was steaming, the brownish grass charred black. It was only the rain beating down that prevented a potential fire. Until a few days ago, that single lightning strike could have burned down half his place. Another reason to be thankful for the rain.

"That was close." Bobby frowned. "Too damn close."

Hayden nodded, his mind made up. "No riding out in that. I know the north fence has taken a beating, but it'll wait." He ran a hand over the back of his neck.

Bobby's gaze narrowed as he studied the singed grass. "Agreed. If we're done here, I'll head home. Surprise the wife."

Hayden nodded. "I'll put everything away. You go on."

Bobby didn't have to be told twice. With a tip of his beaten hat, he was hurrying across the mud to his waiting truck. He and Opal lived in one of the old homesteads on the property. Far enough for privacy, close enough for emergencies—as Bobby put it.

Hayden lifted a hand as the older man drove by, then turned his focus to unloading the back of his truck. Damn Bobby and his chatter. If he'd kept his opinions and his questions to himself, Hayden wouldn't be forced to see things as they were. There was no way around it. He was stubborn but he knew when to throw in the towel. No point fighting a losing battle. When it came to Lizzie, he had lost his heart.

Now all he had to do was figure out what to do about it.

* * *

Sierra wasn't budging. No matter where Lizzie went, the dog was glued to her side. When Lizzie was cooking, Sierra sprawled within reach on the kitchen floor. When she was setting the table, Sierra sat at attention watching her back-and-forth. But now breakfast was over and Lizzie was elbow-deep in a sink of sudsy water and Sierra's chocolate brown gaze remained glued her way. If Lizzie didn't know better, she'd think Sierra was hoping for a dropped bit of toast or bacon. But she did know better. Sierra was doing her job—being there for Lizzie.

"You're a good girl," she said to the dog, making Sierra wag her tail with enthusiasm. "You know it, too. I don't care what Hayden says, I *know* you're smiling at me."

As soon as she said Hayden's name, Charley ran to the back door. *Poor Charley.* Every time she or Jan had mentioned Hayden, Charley had trotted to the back door. Now the poor dog sat staring out the window so hard it seemed like he was trying to will Hayden's return.

"He'll be back soon," Lizzie said, hoping she was right.

Since both Jan and Weston were taking a nap, Lizzie headed to her bedroom. Silly or not, she wanted to pull herself together before Hayden got home. Sierra followed, sitting on the bath mat as Lizzie showered.

Lizzie tugged on the yoga pants and bright safety-yellow Granite Falls Rodeo T-shirt Jan had offered her. *Bright* was an understatement. *Neon* was more like it.

She frowned at her reflection. Between the near dress-sized neon T-shirt and her humidity-wild hair, she didn't look in the least bit pulled together. "Whatever," she murmured, twisting her hair up and tying it into a bun. "Working with what we have."

Sierra sat up, her tail wagging.

"I'll take that as agreement." She stooped, running a hand along Sierra's head before they left her bedroom and headed down the hallway.

Weston's nursery door was open so she peeked inside. "No Weston," she said to Sierra. He'd been pretty wide-eyed after breakfast, some hide-and-seek around the couch, and his favorite, stacking blocks and then knocking them down. "Weston?" she called. Maybe he was hiding in his room.

He must have fussed enough for Jan to take him with her.

The hair on the back of her neck went up as soon as she reached the living room. The back door was wide open. Her heart rate began to climb.

No sign of Jan and Weston on the back porch. Which was good, considering the amount of rain and thunder and lightning rolling off the black clouds outside.

Maybe Hayden was home.

But he wouldn't use the back door—he'd park in the shop and come through the side door…

Charley?

She stepped forward, ready to close the back door, when she heard Charley barking. Not just regular barking either—something was wrong. Sierra started whimpering then, taking one look her way, then running out into the rain.

Something is very wrong.

"Jan?" she called out, her heart in her throat. It took seconds to run down the hall, knock on her door and open it.

"Lizzie?" Jan asked, her voice thick with sleep.

"Weston…" She was running before she could think. Weston. Hayden had called him "the escape artist," said he was becoming a speed walker. *No.* She remembered his little leg thrown over the edge of the crib when she'd walked in… Her heart was on the verge of imploding then, beating so hard it was the only sound she could hear. She ran outside, slipping when her feet hit the rain-slicked grass— but she kept going. Nothing could stop her. Not the thunder overhead or the splash of the puddles beneath her bare feet. She strained to hear Charley— to hear Sierra—following the sound of their barking as quickly as possible.

Twice she slipped on the mud and went down. *No, no, no.* She didn't have time for this. Weston didn't have time for this. She pushed herself up and kept going, wiping the rain from her eyes and stumbling over rocks and ruts in the ground beneath her.

She was crying, she couldn't help it. It didn't matter. Nothing mattered. She had to find him, had to hold his giggling, soft body close. She had to. She would find him. *Weston.* Every bark had her moving faster—desperate to reach them.

Finally, she saw Charley. He was staying close to an old metal storage shed. The dog was circling something, ears and tail up. Sierra was there too, moving in the opposite direction. As if they were herding something. Or someone. *Please, please...*

Their barking turned frantic when they saw her. But over the barking and thunder, she heard the sweetest sound. "Weston?"

When she reached the shed, Charley and Sierra turned as one—showing her what they'd been working so hard to keep beneath the slight overhang of the shed roof.

"Weston!" she cried, kneeling to scoop the mud-coated toddler into her arms. "Hi, sweetie."

"Hi," he said, then burst into tears, burying his little face against her shoulder.

"I know, baby. I know." She was crying too, her heart on the verge of beating out of her chest. "Charley and Sierra were keeping you safe, weren't they?" His slight weight was heaven in her arms. He was sobbing, but his pudgy little arms were around her neck—he was safe. "You're safe." And she was overcome with pure relief and joy. "It's okay, baby." She smiled, hugging him.

Charley pushed his head against her arm, leaning into her with a rumbly moan.

"You did good, Charley. Such a good boy," she said, including the dog in her embrace. "Thank you for protecting him. Now, let's get home. Okay?" She stood, her feet sinking into the clay mud beneath her bare feet. "We are all getting a bath when we get home."

Weston patted her chest with one hand, his cries softening. "Hi."

"Hi to you, too." She pressed a kiss to the top of his head, uncaring that he was fully covered in mud. "Home. Let's go home."

"'Kay," he mumbled, turning his face against her chest as she set off, moving as quickly as the rain-soaked earth would allow, back to the ranch house. Thankfully, she had Charley and Sierra to help. Every few steps, one or the other of them would come back to her, wait for her to catch up, then run a few steps ahead.

It was slow going—there was no help for it.

The storm raged on, shaking the ground and drenching her, but she didn't blink. Nothing— absolutely nothing—could compare to the fear she'd had over losing Weston. Nothing. But he was okay. She was okay. No, she was good. *Take that.* She glared up at the sky. *You can't scare me anymore.*

Weston's little hand twined in her hair.

"Charley is taking us home," she said, her eyes trained on Sierra's white coat. "Almost there." She hoped. When she'd run out of the house, she hadn't exactly been paying attention to where she was going. Now she'd have to count on the dogs to get them home. "Home. Bath. And nap. And maybe some yum yums, too." She kept chattering, nonsense really, hoping to calm Weston amid the roar of the storm overhead.

When the house came into view, Lizzie wanted to cry all over again. This time from relief. "Home, Weston," she said. "See?"

Weston lifted his head. "Da da da da!"

Hayden. Lizzie nodded, her heart picking up for entirely different reasons now. "Yes, baby, I see him." She closed her eyes, sucking in a deep breath, the adrenaline that had carried her through beginning to ebb.

Hayden and Jan were on the back porch talking, arms flailing and voices raised but indistinguishable. Until he saw them. He was running toward them, sheer terror on his face.

"He's coming," she whispered, her throat suddenly tight.

Hayden jumped the back fence, splashed through a massive puddle and didn't stop until he had his hands on them.

"He's okay." She nodded, staring up at Hayden. "He's a mess, but he's okay."

"Da da," Weston said, leaning toward his father before dissolving into another bout of tears. "Da."

Hayden's gaze swept over her face before he cradled his son against his chest. For an instant, the anguish on his face tore at her heart. Then his arms were steel bands about her—around them, his breath escaping from his chest in broken, trembling bursts. "Thank you." Two words that revealed all the fear and panic this big, beautiful man was feeling.

"He's okay," she said again, needing to reassure him. Because she loved him. She loved him without doubt or hesitation. Being wrapped up in his arms, held tight, was like coming home...

Weston's pat on her shoulder made her smile. She caught his little hand and pressed a kiss to his palm. He giggled, resting his head against Hayden's chest.

With one arm around her shoulders, Hayden steered them toward shelter. It was only when they stood, dripping mud and sludge onto the Spanish tile beneath her bare feet, that he let go of her.

"Lizzie, honey, thank you." Jan pulled her into a hard embrace. "Thank you so much."

She nodded, words failing her now. Instead, she hugged Jan back—doing her best not to fall apart on the woman.

"Your face." Jan was saying, wiping the tears from her cheeks. "I've never been so scared in all my life. But you didn't stop… You took off. Went after him."

Lizzie nodded, fearful of the sharp stinging in her eyes.

Jan held her by the shoulders, staring her straight in the eye. "Without a moment's hesitation."

"I had to…" She broke off, clearing her throat when her words wavered.

Jan tugged her in for another hug. "It's all right now."

It was—so why were tears streaming down her face? Weston was home. They were safe. And the storm shaking the glass in their panes? Nothing.

"Mom." Hayden's voice, gruff and deep and wonderful.

"Ni ni ni." Weston's voice was cheerful. "Hi hi."

"You come right here to your Nini, Weston." Jan's arms fell away. "Boy howdy, does someone need a bath. Maybe then we can make sure you still have all of your fingers and toes under all this mud."

Lizzie wrapped her arms around herself, loving the smile on little Weston's face. It wasn't hard to accept that she loved this little boy as if he were her own. She did. Looking at Hayden was another matter altogether. If she did, he'd know… And she wasn't ready to tell him she loved him, with all her heart.

But then she was enveloped in his arms. Hayden. His scent, his warmth, his breath against her ear. She melted into him, a broken moan slipping free before she could stop it. The way he held her—fierce and protective—broke her restraint. She hadn't wanted to cry on him but now she was sobbing, hard. His arms tightened, his hands pressing against her back, holding her in place. With the thundering of his heart beneath her ear drowning out the thunder of the storm outside, it was tempting to imagine a future with this man.

"Thank you, Lizzie." His voice was gruff, his breath warm against her neck.

She nodded, staring up at him. "Don't thank me. Hayden, I had to go after him." She swallowed. "I love him… How could I not? All that mattered was getting to him. Making sure he was safe."

His gaze bore into hers, his hands steady against her back. "And he is. Because of you. You're so damn brave, Lizzie Vega."

Was she? It hadn't been about bravery. It had been instinct. But now? Maybe she would be brave, after all. "And I…" Her voice wavered and her breath was a sort of hiccup but the words forced their way out. "I…I love you too, Hayden. I do."

He stiffened, his gaze falling from hers and his jaw locking tight.

Her heart twisted sharply, hurt pressing from the inside out. She didn't have the strength to be brave anymore. Somehow, she managed to pull away from him, hurry to the privacy of her room and give in to her tears with Sierra at her side.

Chapter Fifteen

Hayden poured a cup of water over his son's bare stomach, chuckling at Weston's gleeful laughter. Right now, he couldn't take his eyes off Weston. Every few seconds, he gave one of his son's chubby feet a squeeze. Anything to erase the soul-crushing seconds between learning Weston was missing and seeing Lizzie, triumphant and smiling, with Weston in her arms. That moment… Well, his poor heart had stopped, broken, then jump-started in the span of a few minutes. He gave Weston's big toe a tickle. "You're my little fish," he said. "A fish in the bath."

Weston nodded. "Baf."

"I know you like your bath." He smiled, amazed

at how quickly Weston's vocabulary was growing. "You like water."

Weston nodded again. "Baf."

"You need any help?" his mother asked, peering around the bathroom door.

Hayden shook his head. "I think we're just about done here." He glanced her way, weighing the risks of asking, then asking anyway, "How is Lizzie?" Having her push free of his arms and run to the guest room had gutted him. He'd been hard-pressed not to go after her—he couldn't. As much as his arms ached to hold her, to assure himself that she was fine, he knew it would break his resolve and he'd pour out his heart to her. Neither of them needed that.

"I can't say, Hayden." His mother came into the room and leaned against the counter. "She's still in her room. Pretty shaken up, of course. We all are."

But he knew the whole truth of it. Lizzie hadn't just saved his son, she'd had to face her greatest fear to do so. For Weston. He didn't know what to do or say to make her understand how grateful he was. There were no words. None he could say, anyway.

The vision popped up again. Lizzie and Weston, covered in mud—

He sucked in a deep breath and turned to Weston. Safe and sound and splashing in his bath. Because of Lizzie. His heart thumped. "If she hadn't…" He broke off, unable to finish that thought, let alone say the words out loud.

"She did." His mother's hand rested on his shoulder. "It all turned out just fine, Hayden. Thanks to her."

"Lizzie had told me about Weston… Told me he'd been trying to climb out of his crib." And he'd forgotten. "Today is my fault."

"Hayden, today was no one's fault." His mother sighed. "And it's all over now."

If that were true, he wouldn't feel so damn guilty. But he did. Hayden nodded, Charley leaning against his side. He gave the dog a pat.

"I'll go get some dinner started, okay?" she asked. "Give Lizzie a break from taking care of everything." She patted his shoulder before heading to the door.

Weston clapped his hands and splashed the water, dousing Hayden's shirtfront and Charley's head.

"I need a bath too, huh?" Hayden asked.

Weston giggled as Charley shook his head.

"You three are sure making a mess. Best mop that up so no one slips and hurts themselves." But his mother was smiling when she left.

"Nini can sure be bossy sometimes." He shook his head.

"Ni ni ni," Weston said, slapping the water again.

By the time his bath was done, Weston was squeaky clean and Hayden was dripping wet. Not that he minded. He wrapped Weston in a hooded towel and carried him down the hall—Charley trailing along. He paused at Lizzie's door before moving on to the nursery.

"We'll get you dressed and see what Nini has cooked up for dinner." Hayden dressed Weston. "But first, I need you to show me how you got out." He pressed a kiss to Weston's forehead and put his son in his crib. "I'm going to wait right outside."

Weston bounced, smiling broadly. "Da da."

"I'll be right out here, little man," he said, leaving the door wide open. If he was going to do this right, he needed to see his son in action. Weston gazed his way with wide light brown eyes. He waved, then proceeded to try a happy game of peekaboo. Hayden grinned, stepping out of Weston's immediate view.

His gaze slid to Lizzie's door, his heart in his throat. He was tempted to knock. And say what? He rested his head against the wall and waited. First things first. And that meant keeping his son from repeating today's little episode. He marveled at the fact that Weston had gone from unsteady on his own feet to master escape artist in a matter of weeks. His boy was smart. And quick.

Lizzie's door opened. She stepped out, saw him and froze.

For a split second he was frozen, too. *I love you too, Hayden. I do.* Hearing those words… He'd wanted them to be true. Those hazel-green eyes of hers fell away from his but it didn't stop his heart from thumping hard against his chest.

"Everything okay?" she asked softly.

It did look suspicious—almost like he was waiting on her. "I'm spying on Weston," he said, nodding at the door. "I put him in his crib," he explained, pulling Weston's door closed. "Trying to re-create the little guy's escape."

She nodded but she didn't look up or say anything.

He stared at the top of her bent head, tongue-tied and flustered. From an early age, he'd been one to sift through scenarios, weigh pros and cons, and be deliberate when choosing a course of action. With Lizzie, he was split. The logical side couldn't accept that this thing between them could survive outside of this sheltered, secluded world they'd created over the last few days. In the real world? What chance did they stand? The less logical, more emotional side he hadn't been all that in touch with a few days ago? That side wanted to drag her into his arms and never let her go. When it came to Lizzie, he had a lot of wants.

Say something. He cleared his throat, drawing her gaze his way.

But he was still trying to come up with what he wanted to say when Weston opened his bedroom door and stood there smiling.

"That didn't take long." Lizzie knelt, holding out her hands. "You're a little Houdini, aren't you?"

Weston giggled his way into her arms. "Li Li."

He patted her chest, then twined his arms around her neck.

The look on Lizzie's face… Whatever air was left in Hayden's lungs was gone. She looked like, maybe, she did love his boy. *Really* loved him. Hayden watched the exchange, his heart swelling up and making his chest tight. "Li Li, huh?" he asked, the question gruff and low.

Lizzie scooped Weston up, cradling him with true affection. "Is that me?" She smiled, bouncing him against her hip. "Am I Li Li?"

Weston patted her in affirmation. "Li Li." His mother was right—his son was definitely smitten with Lizzie.

"I like that." She wrinkled up her nose, sniffing hard and repeating, "I like that a lot, Weston." Her hazel eyes met his for a split second before turning back to Weston.

Silence fell long enough for the light pitter-patter of rain on the roof to be heard. "Still raining." Her voice was soft but Hayden didn't detect the usual underlying panic. "Rain, rain, go away," she sang. "Baby Weston wants to play." She tapped the tip of Weston's nose and earned a giggle.

"It's letting up. By morning, it will be gone." The thought caused a jagged lump to lodge in his throat.

"How soon do you think we'll be able to get to the base and then my car?" she asked.

He cleared his throat, swallowed, but the damn

lump stuck. "Maybe tomorrow." Too soon. No—not soon enough. The longer she stayed, the more it would hurt. "With today's rainfall, it's hard to know for sure."

A large rattle from the kitchen had Lizzie turning. "Sounds like Nini is cooking. Should we go see if she needs help?" She carried Weston down the hall and into the great room without looking back.

He ran his hand along the back of his neck, blew out a long slow breath, then headed into the nursery. With any luck, lowering the mattress would keep Weston safely inside. But, just to be sure, he located one of the doorknob covers for the inside of Weston's nursery door. "Looks good," he said to Charley.

Charley's tail wagged.

"Glad you agree." He sighed, giving Charley's back a pat. "Wish everything was as easy to take care of." He tucked the screwdriver into his back pocket and flipped off the nursery light, then headed to the kitchen.

Lizzie was sitting in a recliner reading a board book to Weston, who was resting comfortably on her lap. He paused midway across the room to listen in, doing his best to look preoccupied with a pile of papers on the end table.

"The cows and pigs." Lizzie paused. "See, that's a cow. And there's the pig." She glanced at Weston, who smiled up at her. "The horses and sheep. Horse," she said, pointing at the picture. "And sheep."

Weston tapped the picture, babbling. "Hee and shee and caw."

"Yes." Lizzie smiled. "Horse and sheep and cow." She ran her fingers through the wisp of light brown hair on the top of Weston's head. With a broad smile on her face, she looked up and their gazes collided.

He wasn't sure what got him more, the flash in her eyes or the way his son reached up to gently grasp one of Lizzie's long curls. Might be that it was both things together. One thing was certain—there was nothing he wanted more. Long after she left, she'd be in his heart.

"That was delicious, Jan." Lizzie stood. "I'll take cleanup duty."

"You don't have to do that," Jan argued. "Hayden can."

Lizzie loved the way the corner of Hayden's mouth cocked up, the way one brow rose high. Then again, she loved everything about him. "He's had cleanup duty on the dogs and Weston. I've got this covered." If she didn't do something, she'd keep replaying her embarrassing declaration—and Hayden's silence. "It's the least I can do before I go when you've all been so good to me."

Hayden stood, his eyes locking with hers. "I'll help."

Which was the exact opposite of what she wanted.

"Jan, I think there's some leftover apple pie. I know Weston liked it."

"I won't say no to pie." Jan smiled. "What about you, Weston? More yum yum?"

Weston grinned.

Lizzie laughed, busying herself with collecting dessert plates and serving up pie while doing her best not to react to Hayden taking up the space at the sink right behind her. "Want some, Hayden?" she asked, smiling at Charley and Sierra as they waited, ever hopeful that some of tonight's dinner would fall on the floor.

"Maybe later." He eyed the plate, then her, his gaze falling to her mouth.

She blinked, the intensity on his face a shock. "Okay," she mumbled, all but tripping over her own feet as she served Jan her pie.

Weston's whole face lit up, his little hands reaching forward as Jan put some cinnamon apple pieces on the tray of his high chair.

Lizzie picked up Jan's and Weston's dinner dishes and carried them to Hayden.

"Thanks." He reached for them.

She held the plates back. "You've done your fair share."

He stepped aside, leaning against the kitchen counter and wiping his hands on a kitchen towel with embroidered bluebonnet trim work. "Guess I'll stand by."

She shot him a look. "Have some pie. I've got this." *Please, please don't stand there looking at me.*

"I'll wait. Have some with you later." There was that look again—that breath-stealing, nerve-tingling look that held all sorts of secrets and promise.

And just like that, she was aching for him. "Okay." Her voice wobbled and she almost dropped the plate she was rinsing. Hayden reached around her, catching it before it hit the granite countertop, but those light brown eyes never left hers.

"See." The corner of his mouth kicked up.

All she could *see* was him. His warmth. His clean scent. His smile. And those beautiful, searching eyes.

"Bet you're glad I was on stand-by now." He was teasing but his tone was edged with a delicious gruffness.

Instead of answering him, she shot him another *whatever* look and went back to rinsing off the dishes and loading them into the dishwasher. It might have been her imagination, but he seemed keenly focused on her neck…

"I think this little guy is about done for the night," Jan said. "No surprise, after the day's events."

The day's events. The words had her replaying everything in slow motion—from discovering Weston's empty crib to running into the rain to carrying him home. Yes, home. She risked another look Hayden's way.

His jaw muscle was locked tight and his knuckles whitened as he gripped the edge of the counter-top. Covering his hand with hers was instinctual. She knew what he was thinking, if not what he was feeling. He was Weston's father after all—the depths of his fear and panic were beyond comprehension.

She hadn't expected him to catch her hand in his. The slide of his fingers, threading with hers. The brush of his thumb along the back of her hand and the flat of her palm before sliding free. Innocent-enough touches. So why was she leaning against the kitchen counter, her heart hammering away?

His gaze slammed into hers then and held.

She was vaguely aware of Jan talking but she was too caught up in Hayden to hear a word the woman was saying. Something about bed. Lack of an after-noon nap. How late it was… But the words *I'll put him to bed* snapped Lizzie out of it.

"Would it be okay if I put him to bed?" Lizzie asked, hearing just how high-pitched and strained she sounded. She swallowed and tried again. "If I leave tomorrow… It sounds silly but I know I'm going to miss Weston." The second she'd said the words, an unbearable pressure sat on her chest.

Hayden was staring at the floor, his jaw muscle bulging now.

"Of course, Lizzie." Jan was looking between the two of them, a slight furrow between her brows as she joined them in the kitchen with Weston in her arms. "I have to say, I'm not ready for those roads to be open yet. Not ready for you to leave us, that's for sure." Jan touched Lizzie's cheek, then gave her a quick hug. "I've said it before and I'll say it again. You're always welcome."

Weston clapped his hands. "Li Li," he said before leaning toward her, arms outstretched.

"I've got you." She hugged Weston close, rubbing noses with the baby smiling up at her.

It was impossible to miss the sharp contrast between her time here and the solitary life she lived in Houston. The life that was waiting for her. She'd told Hayden how she felt... He hadn't said a thing. He definitely hadn't asked her to stay. The pressure increased, a cold ache taking residence in the pit of her stomach. "You don't mind, Hayden?" she asked, deciding not to look at him this time.

"No." He pushed off the counter.

"Let's go, then," Lizzie said, bouncing Weston on their way to his room. She changed his diaper, turned off the overhead light and sat in the rocking chair. "Let's read *It's Time for Bed* tonight, okay, Weston?" Weston was already drooping against her. "'It's time for bed,' said mother mouse." She read softly, smiling at the whimsical illustrations of animal mothers tucking their children into bed. Weston's body was heavy with sleep long before they'd finished the book but Lizzie read through it all, loath to put him in his bed and end this time with him.

"You know what?" she whispered as they rocked.

"You're a special little boy, Weston. You hold a very special place in my heart, that's for sure. You always will." She continued rocking and patting his little back. "You have your Nini, and Charley, and you have the very best daddy who loves you more than anything. And I will miss you, all of you, very much." She stood slowly, carrying him to his crib, and carefully laid him down. Long lashes rested against round, pink cheeks. The slight wisp of hair on his head curled softly. His little rose-petal lips parted and his even breathing filled the nursery. He was the sweetest baby, all smiles and giggles.

And she really would miss him desperately when she left.

She tiptoed from the room, waited for Sierra to join her, then closed the nursery door as quietly as possible. When she returned to the kitchen, it was empty. On the kitchen counter were two dessert plates, each with a sizable piece of pie. Beneath the plates was the *Granite Falls Gazette*. The newspaper had been folded to the employment opportunities with the open position at the new Granite Falls High School. This time, a bright red circle had been added on top of the yellow highlighter. Lizzie read over the posting, trailing a finger over the newsprint.

"He go down okay?" Hayden's deep voice surprised her.

Hand to her chest, she turned. "You shouldn't sneak up on someone like that."

"Did I?" he asked, offering her one plate and taking the other. "I thought we had a pie date?"

She took the plate, reading over the job posting once more.

"Want to sit on the back porch?" he asked. "The skies are clear and the moon is bright."

He was right. The sky was a velvety midnight blue with stars for miles and the moon a startling white.

"It's incredible." She stared, in awe. "Houston rarely has clear nights. But, when we do, it's nothing like this." Houston was a big city—with city lights bright enough to take some of the shine off the night stars. "Talk about nature's beauty."

"The view never gets old, that's for sure."

She joined him on the wicker love seat, picking at her pie with her fork. "I imagine it doesn't."

They enjoyed their pie in comfortable silence. It was quiet, peacefully so. The steady whir of crickets, the occasional hoot of an owl and the distant mooing of the cattle in the fields beyond—but not much else. Charley sat staring out into the dark while Sierra sprawled at her feet. There was no sense of urgency, just calm. It was near perfect. And tomorrow, she would leave. She hadn't meant to sigh.

But he noticed. "That was some sigh."

She smiled, then shrugged.

"Lizzie, I need to apologize… Today, I mean." He set his empty plate on the porch. "You tried to warn me. If I'd listened to you, I'd have fixed his damn crib and none of this would have happened. None of it. It was my fault—all of it. I can never repay you for what you did."

"You don't need to thank me, Hayden." She waved his words away.

"I do," he argued, grabbing her hand. "Weston is my whole world…"

"I know. I know he is." She stared at their joined hands. "Today was… Well, today was terrifying." She broke off, shaking her head. "But I didn't care about the rain or the thunder or the lightning or anything except finding him. When I saw Charley, heard him bark—and then I saw Weston…" When had she started crying?

Hayden pulled her into his arms then, his breath coming in harsh bursts. "It's over now."

She let him draw her closer—moving closer still. "Once I was holding him, I knew everything was going to be okay." She sniffed, turning her face into his chest. Breathing him deep, drawing in his scent and warmth. "Not just Weston, though that was most important… But me, too."

"I know. Seeing you two… Seeing you. I could tell you'd faced your fears and kicked ass." His words were part growl, part rasp. He tugged her closer, until she was half in and half out of his lap, wrapped up in him.

Lizzie closed her eyes, listening to Hayden's heart. It was fast. Not quite rabbit speed, but fast nonetheless. His hands twisted in her shirt, anchoring her there with a sense of desperation that demanded a response. How could she ever resist him? Why would she want to?

"And I'm forever grateful." His voice was gruff. "I know there is no way I can ever return the favor—"

"Maybe you can." She was gripping his shirtfront when she looked up at him.

"Name it." He searched her face, one hand smoothing the hair from her shoulder. "What can I do?"

"Two things." Her heart was definitely creeping toward rabbit speed. One more night. That was all they had. "Kiss me." She held her breath, hoping—

There was nothing restrained or tentative about his kiss. His mouth met hers and melted every bone in her body. She was straining against him, moaning from the brush of his tongue along the seam of her lips and gasping when their breaths mingled, hot and ragged.

He pulled back, breathing hard. "What's the second thing?"

Her nerves almost got the best of her. Almost. But the hunger in his kiss gave her the courage to say, "Stay with me tonight."

He groaned. "I was hoping you were going to say that."

The trip from the back porch to his bed was a blur. She was caught up in the hungry slide of his hands and the desperation of his lips clinging to hers. Each touch demanded another. One kiss turned into two, which turned into many more kisses, longer, harder, each more frantic than the last. When every stitch of clothing had been tossed aside and they met, skin to skin, he paused to cradle her cheeks, to smooth the hair from her face and search her eyes. They fell back on his bed, his lips soft against hers as he slid inside her. Gazes locked and bodies joined, she lost herself in the overwhelming pleasure Hayden gave to her—in the love she had for him.

Chapter Sixteen

Hayden smoothed the dark curls from Lizzie's face. Since she was sound asleep, he could look his fill— so he did. Her full lips were parted. Long, dark lashes rested against her cheek. The sweep of her jaw and the exposed arch of her neck. His fingers itched to touch her. Again. He'd never been this fascinated by another person, never wanted to learn every dip and curve of someone's body. With Lizzie, he couldn't get enough. Now the sun was creeping through his window and, even though he'd had next to no sleep, he wasn't ready for a new day to begin.

Not if it meant she was leaving.

He hadn't meant to eavesdrop but, with Weston's

monitor on his dresser, there was no way he'd missed her words. There was no denying she loved his son. But loving him? He stared down at her, doing his best to burn this memory into his brain.

I do love you, Lizzie Vega. Watching her leave was going to be brutal.

There was a slight birthmark on the curve of her shoulder. A starburst. *Fitting.* He grinned. She'd burst into his life. There was no other way to put it. And, in his eyes, she shone just as brightly as the stars overhead. Her leaving…

He pressed his eyes shut and lay back, his arm pillowing his head.

He ticked off all the reasons to stay quiet. Her job. Her home. But, above everything, the need to make her mother proud. If he asked, he'd be asking her to make a choice between honoring her mother's memory and staying with him. He wouldn't do that. He couldn't.

He ran a hand over his face.

The time they'd shared was here, wrapped up in each other and safe. How could that last when they went back to their respective worlds. Maybe then, when they were apart, they'd know if this could be real and lasting. He sighed.

"You're awfully restless." Lizzie's hand was soft against his chest. "Everything okay?"

He took a long look at Lizzie. Her hair was mussed and her eyes mossy green and heavy with sleep. She was awake—which meant he could touch her. He rolled back onto his side, trailing his fingers along the side of her face, along her neck and down the slope of her shoulder.

A small, sleepy smile turned up the corners of her mouth. "Good morning," she whispered.

He nodded. Best morning he'd had in… Well, he couldn't remember. No telling when, or if, he'd feel this way again. He ignored the sharp tug in his chest, the tightening around his heart. "Morning." His voice was far harsher than he'd intended.

Her smile faded as her eyes focused on his face. The longer she studied him, the heavier the air became. The attraction was there, electric as ever, but this was something else.

"Da da da." Weston's voice broke the weighted silence of the room. "Da da."

Lizzie's face eased into a smile. "I think you're being paged." But then she sat up. "Which means I need to hurry so your mom doesn't catch me."

The horrified expression on her face had him laughing.

"It's not funny." She frowned, tugging on the Army Mom shirt and too-big athletic pants she'd borrowed. "I don't want her to think I'm…I'm…" She frowned. "I mean, we did… And I've only been here, what?" She swallowed, looking more and more horrified.

"It doesn't matter." His hands settled on her shoulders. "It feels like you've…always been here." It was hard to get the last words past the lump in his throat.

She stared up at him, her mouth opening, then closing.

Weston was singing now, his voice rising and falling.

"That's my cue." His hands slowly slid from her shoulders, down her arms, to caress over her hands and fingers before letting her go. Without another look, he left her standing in his bedroom. If he stayed one second longer, all his good intentions would go out the window. He'd ask her to stay. Hell, might even beg.

"Da da," Weston said, his smile as bright as the sun.

"Good to see you're still in your bed." He reached down to scoop Weston into his arms. "How's my boy?" he asked, pressing a kiss to his son's forehead.

"Da da, Ni ni, yum yum." Weston played with his toes while Hayden changed his diaper. "Li Li?" Weston asked, glancing toward the nursery door? "Li Li," he called.

The lump in Hayden's throat went from uncomfortable to painful. But he smiled as he changed Weston's pajamas for some jeans and a shirt that read Cowboy in Training. He nodded. "You look good." He knelt, letting Weston walk with him. "Let's get some breakfast. We'll see what the day has in store." With any luck, the roads would still be closed.

Weston was quick on his feet. He squealed with glee when Charley greeted him with a tail wag and a full-body sniff. Sierra was more subdued. She sat, letting Weston give her happy pats. "Do-gee," he said, patting Charley now.

"Right you are." Hayden nodded. "Charley." He pointed at Charley. "And Sierra." Sierra's tail wagged.

Weston looked back and forth between the dogs. "Do-gee." He nodded.

Hayden chuckled. "Right."

"Morning." His mother was awful chipper this morning. "Coffee ready?"

"Making it now." He measured out the coffee grounds and water and turned the machine on. "Feeling good this morning?"

She nodded. "I am." She lowered her voice. "I made a call this morning."

He crossed his arms over his chest. "Why do I get the feeling I'm not going to like what you're about to say?"

"I have no idea." She frowned. "Does that mean you don't want to know?"

He sighed. "Go on."

"I spoke with Lanie Davis, you know that poor girl that works at the school district office?" She didn't wait for an answer. "Anyway, I told her about Lizzie and I guess Superintendent Harvey heard because he got on the phone and asked me all sorts of questions—"

"Mom." He cut her off, beyond frustrated. "Why did you do that?"

Confusion lined his mother's face. "Why? Because you—"

"She's not staying." He sighed, turning away from his mother to pour them both a cup of coffee. "She doesn't want to give up her life—her career—for some backwater small town, Mom."

"You asked her, then?" his mother pushed.

He handed her a cup of coffee. "Let's drop it."

"Hayden." His mother covered his hand with hers. "Honey, you've never been one to give up on something you want. Now's not the time."

He kept his mouth shut. This was different. This wasn't just about him and what he wanted. Lizzie had come here to get her life back together, not give it up for something else altogether. Now she could go back with her head held high. It was important that she return to her position, prove to herself that she could do this. He wanted that for her, wanted her to do whatever she wanted with renewed confidence. After yesterday—with Weston... Well, she'd earned that.

"Li Li," Weston said, running-wobbling across the tile floor.

Hayden watched, his heart thumping as she scooped up Weston and rubbed noses with him.

"Good morning, Weston." She was smiling as she added, "Good morning."

"Good morning," his mother said. "How are you this bright and sunshiny day?"

Lizzie glanced out the back windows. Maybe he was imagining things but, for a second, there was a flash of disappointment on her face. "It's a beautiful day," she said, bouncing Weston on her hip. "Do we know about the roads?" She was still looking out the back windows.

"Well…" Jan sighed. "Looks like Hayden can get his truck through there. Where is your car?"

"At the Quik N' Go." He hoped like hell they didn't hear the disappointment twisting up his insides.

His mother turned, her face pinched. "Should be good after lunch."

"Well…" He cleared his throat. "That's good news." Might be but it didn't feel like it—not to him, anyway. "We can head out when Weston goes down for his nap." He risked a glance her way.

She was still studying Weston. "Yes. That sounds like a plan." Her tone was flat.

"Lizzie." His mother was up, crossing to her. "Hayden has informed me that I overstepped but I made a phone call this morning—"

"Mom," he barked.

"Shush, Hayden. It's done. She might as well know." His mother frowned at him, her hands on her hips. "I spoke with Superintendent Harvey, the man who's in charge of the hiring and firing for the Granite Falls district." She paused, ignoring him altogether. "He would be very interested in looking at your résumé. He says there are a whole bunch of parents who want to add some dual-credit classes—something about getting college credit or something?"

"Oh? Really…" Lizzie glanced his way, then back at his mother. "Well, I'm touched that you reached out to him." Her eyes met his and held.

"I told her you wouldn't be interested. You've got a life and a job to get back to." He cleared his throat. "You've been stuck here long enough." Like a fool, he held his breath—waiting for her to say something that would give him the slightest glimmer of hope. *Because I'm a damn fool.*

"I hope you'll think about it." His mother patted Lizzie on the cheek. "I know you've only been here a short time but, well, I like having you around. I know I'm not the only one."

He didn't miss the pointed look his mother shot his way. But, lucky for him, Lizzie assumed she was talking about Weston.

"You'll miss me?" Lizzie asked, rubbing noses with Weston again. "Well, you know what? I will miss you, too." The waver in her voice was a kick to the gut.

Hayden wasn't sure he was prepared for the hell

of her leaving. Since she was leaving today, he'd better start getting ready.

The tension in the truck cab was so thick, it made it hard to breathe. Lizzie kept fiddling with the trim of her embroidered tunic and smoothing the layered gauze skirts, fighting a whole new sort of panic. She had to keep reminding herself that Hayden was right. She had a life to get back to. Besides, she didn't want to stay someplace she wasn't wanted. She'd laid all of her cards out there and it hadn't mattered. Hayden might be attracted to her but he didn't love her.

Wasn't there a movie that said relationships that started under stressful circumstances never lasted? She couldn't remember the name but Sandra Bullock was in it. *How is that relevant?*

No one fell in love that fast. She didn't believe in soul mates... Before.

Before what? There was no point in asking—she knew the answer. *Hayden Mitchell is not my soul mate.*

But there was a tiny voice, one that was growing louder and louder with every passing mile. What if he is? What if all of this had happened because this place was where she belonged? Her mother wanted her to be successful—and happy. Her work at the university was just that: work.

Being here... She'd never been so happy. The idea of losing him hurt too much.

You are too strong, too fierce a woman be ruled by fear.

Grammy's words.

She glanced at Hayden.

His hands gripped the steering wheel, knuckled white and posture ramrod stiff. His jaw was clenched tight. While she wanted to read all sorts of things into his distant behavior, the chances that he would have somehow come to feel as intensely for her as she had for him were… She shrugged. *Slim. Not in my favor.*

They pulled through the gates of the base annex and drove the final stretch to the K-9 Center. Her heart was beating so loudly there was no way he couldn't hear it. If he did, he didn't let on.

He parked the truck, rolled down the windows and climbed down. "You two stay put," he said to Sierra and Charley. "We're coming right back." He came around the truck, holding out his hand to help her down.

The instant her hand met his, it was the same. A zap of electrical current, drawing them together and fine-tuning her awareness of the man in front of her. Standing there, her sandal-clad feet sinking in the mud, all she could do was stare at their hands.

He was looking at her, she could feel it.

But if she looked up and stared into those light brown eyes. She'd do something she regretted—say something ridiculous and make a complete fool out of herself. Hadn't she done that enough already? Yes, she had. So…

What do I have to lose?

Hayden. Her heart. Weston. The sense of belonging and family and…well, everything.

"Your shoes," he said, stepping back, letting go of her hand and walking quickly to the door of the K-9 Center.

She followed, slipping off her sandals and following him inside. *You're a confident independent woman. You go after what you want.* She drew in a deep breath. *I can do this.*

"Phone's probably dead," he said, holding out her purse. "Probably want to charge it before you get on the road, just in case."

"Yes." She nodded. "Wouldn't want to slide off a bridge without a working phone…" It was a pathetic attempt at a joke—but it was one of the first times she'd made him laugh. "Remember? On the ride out to your house?"

He nodded. His light brown eyes met hers but his smile was strained.

If she didn't say something, she'd never see him again. Of course, he could look at her like she was deranged and that could still wind up happening but… *I can do this.* "I realized something this morning." Her heart was pounding away now, her purse clutched to her chest. "What you'd said about returning the favor last night… Has that offer expired or does it still apply?"

His nod was near imperceptible. The rigid angle of his jaw clenched so tight she worried he'd crack a tooth.

"It would help if you weren't scowling at me." She frowned. "Are you mad at me? Did I do something?"

"Lizzie." He ran a hand over his face, muffling his frustrated groan. "No. I'm not mad at you. I'm… sad." His gaze met hers.

She knew, right then and there, everything was going to be okay. The look on his face—the pain in his beautiful eyes. He was sad because she was leaving… Her heart was so full. "One more favor, then…" She swallowed, set her purse on the chair and stepped toward him. "Tell me that I don't love you. That all of this is some sort of time-and-place thing and, when I drive away, what I thought I was feeling for you will disappear."

He stared at the floor, his hands on his hips. "You don't love me, Lizzie. I don't love you. We just… clicked. That's all."

His words cut deep, so deep it hurt to breath. "Of course." He was wrong. It was real. For her, anyway. Otherwise, it couldn't hurt this way.

He nodded but didn't look at her. "This isn't where you belong, Lizzie. You've got what you came for."

He looked at her then. "I won't say it hasn't been nice having you here. It has. It's just—"

"It's time to get back to the real world?" Her eyes stung. She didn't believe him. He cared about her, she knew he did. *He's pushing me away.* "And this isn't the real world." Maybe they should spent a little time apart. Maybe then he'd see that this, they, were the real thing.

"It's not. We both know that." He stepped closer, running one hand over her curls. "But I'm glad we had the time we had."

She nodded, doing her best to smile. "Me too, Hayden." How was she going to walk out of here? *One foot after the other. Easy.* She could do it. "If you're ever in Houston—"

"I'll look you up." He nodded.

"Good." The sooner she was on the road the better. "I should go, then. Don't want Weston to wake up before you get back."

He nodded again, his gaze fixed on her face and his jaw clenched so tight the muscle bulged.

She stood on tiptoe and kissed his cheek. For a minute longer, she drew in his scent, his warmth—and then let him go.

After that, it was a blur. The drive from the K-9 Center to the gas station and her waiting car was horrible and tense. He barely stopped the truck before she and Sierra barreled out, unable to say more goodbyes. Somehow, she and Sierra wound up in her little car heading home. But the miles clicked by and nothing changed.

"We're going to be fine," she said to Sierra.

Maybe if I say it often enough, it will come true.

Chapter Seventeen

Hayden glanced at the University of Houston map in his hands and confirmed the Fine Arts Building's number. The girl in the Help Center said Dr. Vega's classes were wrapping up but he might catch her before she left for the day.

He had to.

It had been five weeks and three days since he'd watched Lizzie's car disappear. He'd done the best he could to forget but…he couldn't. More than that, he didn't want to. He had no plan to burst into her classroom and cause a scene. If she was well and happy, he'd tell her he was here for the stock show. It wasn't true. The ranch was clipping along without taking more losses but they weren't in a spot to buy more livestock. Not yet.

Lizzie was the only reason he'd made the drive. Period. He had to see her.

The sun was dipping, casting long shadows along the web of concrete paths leading to the different buildings. It was a big campus—but then, Houston was a big city. With nightmare traffic. He ran a hand along the back of his head, tipping his cowboy hat forward to block out the sinking sun.

Another turn and he was there. The Fine Arts Building. Glass and chrome and grand in a way that Granite Falls' new high school could never be.

He shook his head. There was no chickening out now, dammit. He was here.

He pulled the door open and paused.

The foyer was full of art. Framed sketches, sculptures on pedestals, pottery and things that looked more like carefully stacked pieces of trash than anything.

A group of students was heading to the door so he stopped them.

"I'm looking for Dr. Elizabeth Vega?" he asked.

One of the girls stopped, blinked up at him and smiled. "Oh, wow." She nudged the boy next to her. "He's looking for Dr. Vega."

The boy smiled. "Sure. Dr. Vega should still be in her studio. All the way down that hall, then to the left."

Hayden thanked them, slightly puzzled by their behavior, and headed in the direction he'd sent him.

He peered through the glass pane of the double doors leading into the classroom. More of a workshop than a classroom. Walls lined with shelves full of things he wasn't familiar with. Paint, clay, tools, paintbrushes… From the looks of it, Lizzie had a pretty sweet setup.

He pushed through the door and wandered the room, peering behind shelves, stacks of boxes and huge canvases. Still no Lizzie.

But, on the wall hung several sketches. For the most part, they were crude. But the subjects were recognizable. He stared up at the thick lines, in awe. Charley and Sierra, sprawled in a pile on what had to be his back porch. Weston's face—his boy sound asleep.

He was so caught up in Lizzie's sketches that he hadn't heard the click of Sierra's nails on the concrete floor. It was only when the dog pressed her nose to his hand that he knew she was at his side.

"Hey, Sierra." He crouched, running a hand over the Labrador's snowy head.

"Come to take her back?" Lizzie stood in doorway in the far wall. "I thought there was a no-return policy." Her hazel-green eyes stared at him, a mix of surprise and wariness. Her hair was down. It seemed longer, curlier. Her black T-shirt hugged the curves he'd dreamed of for the last few weeks. Her skirts, a bright pattern of mismatched colors and patterns, hung to her calves. Sandals. Silver toe ring.

Damn. "Good to see you." She had no idea how good it was to see her.

She was still staring, tense and braced for... For what? Did she really think he'd come for Sierra?

"I'm not here for Sierra." He held his hands up.

Lizzie pushed off the door. "She wouldn't go with you, anyway."

"No." He chuckled. "Probably not." He stood, his heart—he was so damn happy. Surely. "How are you?"

"Good." Her gaze darted to her sketches. "Fine."

He turned, staring at the rest of her work. "I had no idea you were this talented." He smiled at the sketch of Weston before moving on to the next one.

He'd come here prepared to leave empty-handed. He'd outright lied to her and hated himself ever since. But if he hadn't, he would have broken right there— begged her to stay. He'd been so damn determined to make sure she made the best choice... A choice that wasn't his to make. *I'm a damn fool.* Now, seeing the careful lines and painstaking detail on the thick paper taped to the wall, he began to hope. "This is..."

"You." But her tone was tense. No, frustrated.

He turned to face her.

Her gaze fell from his and she busied herself at one of the large sinks, washing brushes with barely suppressed aggression. "Did you bring Weston or your mother with you?"

"No." He glanced at the sketch of him—in his hat—then back at her.

"Is this some sort of follow-up service I didn't know about?" A paintbrush slipped from her hands into the sink.

That's when he saw how badly her hands were shaking. There was so much to say. So damn much to explain and apologize for. "Lizzie." In four long strides, he'd closed the distance between them. "I needed to see you."

She stared up at him again. "Why?"

"Because I made a mistake." He cleared his throat. "I let you go."

She blinked.

"I thought I was doing the right thing. And I've regretted it every damn day since you left."

"You told me to go." Her voice was thin and high. "You told me you didn't love me… That it wasn't real. I knew you loved me, Hayden. Why would you push me away?"

"Because I thought I knew what was best for you. I didn't, but you already know that." He ran his fingers along her jaw. "It is real."

She leaned into his touch. "So you…you—"

"Lied." He barked the word. "I figured you'd snap out of it, realize you'd made a mistake, by giving up your career, your life. I didn't want you to walk away from what mattered most only to regret it."

There was anger in her eyes. "You hurt me."

"If I could go back, I would. I'd be honest with you this time. I'd stop trying to make your decisions for you, be selfish—tell you to stay. Beg, if I had to." He cradled her face in his hands. "I'm so sorry I hurt you. I'm sorrier than I can ever say."

"And now?" she asked. "Now you want—"

"You. I love you. I want you in my life—I'll take whatever you're willing to give me. I want you to come home but I understand if you're not ready." He swallowed. "If you need to stay here, I'll make the trip."

"You will?" Those beautiful eyes widened.

"You're worth it." He nodded. "All I want is for you to be happy. I'm hoping I can make you happy. If you're willing to give us a chance."

Lizzie had never been so overwhelmed. Had she dreamed about Hayden showing up, begging for her to love him? Far too often. She'd fallen asleep wrapped up in him. With whispered promises. Featherlight kisses. Even in her dreams, there had been an unshakable certainty that he was hers. And she was, and always would be, his. Then she'd wake up and the hurt and loneliness would roll in until she wondered if he hadn't been right. Their time together, all of it, had been almost too good to be real.

Now, here he was. Really here. Tall and broad and handsome—even more so in that cowboy hat.

He loved her. He was asking for forgiveness.

"Can you forgive me?" His voice wavered. "Will you let me love you?" The raw vulnerability on his face told her more than his words ever could.

"I missed you, Hayden." She stood on tiptoe. "I missed you so much."

The moment their lips touched, Hayden's arms pulled her close. "I missed you."

"*This* is where I belong." She pressed her hand against his cheek. "Right here, in your arms."

"Yes." He said, against her lips, his arms tightening around her. "With me." Another kiss, savoring the taste of her against his mouth. "This time, I'm not letting you go."

"I'm glad to hear it." She smiled, her hands gripping his shirtfront.

"I was so worried about getting in your way. Your mom, making her proud… I get it. I thought you needed time to sort things out and decide what you wanted—without being influenced by what I wanted." He closed his eyes, his hands tightened at her waist.

"I know you meant well, Hayden, but those are choices for me to make."

"Believe me, it won't happen again." He rested his forehead against hers.

"I've had a lot of time to think about that. My mother, I mean." She sighed. "You were right about that, too. She loved me so much. Yes, she wanted me to be successful, but she wanted me to be happy, too."

She smiled up at him. "I was the one who sacrificed one for the other."

He nodded. "Maybe you should try doing both."

"Happy and successful?" She shrugged. "I like the sound of that. Here? Or Granite Falls?" She saw the way his jaw tightened. "No clamming up on me now. I'd really like to hear what you want, Hayden."

"That's up to you. Whatever you decide, we'll figure a way to make it work." His eyes met her. "As long as I have you, Lizzie. You and me and Weston—even my mother. A family. Because you are my family."

She nodded. "Just to make sure—this is real? This is really happening?"

"It is. I love you. And you love me." It sounded more like a question than a statement.

"I love you, Hayden. I love you so much." She smiled, reaching up to cradle his face. "More than I knew I could love someone."

"I'll make sure you never regret it." He tilted her head back. "And I'll make sure you never doubt that I love you."

She stood on tiptoe, tugging his head down for another kiss, but he stopped her.

"What I mean is, we're getting married." He didn't sound confident. He didn't look confident.

"Are you asking? Or telling?" She smiled. "The answer might be different."

"Asking. I know better than to tell to do anything

now." He shook his head. "Besides, I want you to choose me. That's a gift. You are a gift." He blew out a slow breath. "So, Elizabeth Vega, will you marry me?"

"Yes. Yes, I will marry you." She was still smiling when he kissed her. Once. Again. So long and hard, breathing become optional once more. When his lips lifted, she was panting—but oh so happy.

He swept her hair from her shoulder. "I don't like being away from you, Lizzie Vega."

"Then I guess it's a good thing I have the phone number for the superintendent there in Granite Falls." She smiled. "Your mother is determined."

"This time, I don't mind so much." He seemed to be studying her. "You're beautiful."

"You are." She shook her head. "Worth sculpting, remember?"

"I remember. Everything." He smiled.

"Hayden…" She drew in a deep breath. "There is one more teeny-tiny thing you could do to repay me, then."

He grinned. "Go on, I'm waiting."

"Take me home?" She stepped back, taking his hand in hers.

He kissed her hand. "I was hoping that's what you were going to say."

* * * * *

If you enjoyed this story,
be sure to look for the next
Texas Cowboys & K-9s story
by Sasha Summers in September 2021!

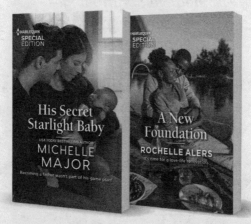

COMING NEXT MONTH FROM

Ⓗ HARLEQUIN
SPECIAL EDITION

#2839 COWBOY IN DISGUISE
The Fortunes of Texas: The Hotel Fortune • by Allison Leigh
Since she first met him months ago in Rambling Rose at the Hotel Fortune, Arabella Fortune has fantasized about sexy and sweet Jay Cross. Now she sets to find out how he'd intended to finish his last words to her: "I think you should know..."

#2840 THE BABY THAT BINDS THEM
Men of the West • by Stella Bagwell
Prudence Keyes and Luke Crawford agree—their relationship is just a fling, even though they keep crossing paths. But an unplanned pregnancy has them reevaluating what they want, even if their past experiences leave both of them a little too jaded to hope for a happily-ever-after.

#2841 STARTING OVER WITH THE SHERIFF
Rancho Esperanza • by Judy Duarte
When a woman who was falsely convicted of a crime she didn't commit finds herself romantically involved with a single-dad lawman, trust issues abound. Can they put aside their relationship fears and come together to create the family they've both always wanted?

#2842 REDEMPTION ON RIVERS RANCH
Sweet Briar Sweethearts • by Kathy Douglass
Gabriella Tucker needed to start over for herself and her kids, so she returned to Sweet Briar, where she'd spent happy summers. Her childhood friend Carson Rivers is still there. Together can they help each other overcome their painful pasts...and maybe find love on the way?

#2843 WINNING MR. CHARMING
Charming, Texas • by Heatherly Bell
Valerie Villanueva moved from Missouri to Charming, Texas, to take care of her sick grandmother. Working for her first love should be easy because she has every intention of going back to her teaching job at the end of summer. Until one wild contest changes everything...

#2844 IN THE KEY OF FAMILY
Home to Oak Hollow • by Makenna Lee
A homestay in Oak Hollow is Alexandra Roth's final excursion before settling in to her big-city career. Officer Luke Walker, her not-so-welcoming host, isn't sure about the "crunchy" music therapist. Yet his recently orphaned nephew with autism instantly grooves to the beat of Alex's drum. Together, this trio really strikes a chord. But is love enough to keep Alex from returning to her solo act?

YOU CAN FIND MORE INFORMATION ON UPCOMING HARLEQUIN TITLES,
FREE EXCERPTS AND MORE AT HARLEQUIN.COM.

HSECNM0521

Since she first met him months ago in Rambling Rose
at the Hotel Fortune, Arabella Fortune has fantasized
about sexy and sweet Jay Cross. Now she sets to find out
how he'd intended to finish his last words to her:
"I think you should know…"

Read on for a sneak peek at
Cowboy in Disguise,
the final book in
The Fortunes of Texas: The Hotel Fortune
by New York Times *bestselling author Allison Leigh!*

"I think you'd better kiss me," she murmured, and her cheeks turned rosy.

"Yeah?" His voice dropped also.

"If you don't, then I'll know this is just a dream."

"And if I do?"

She moistened her lips. "Then I'll know this is just a dream."

He smiled slightly. He brushed the silky end of her ponytail against her cheek and leaned closer. "Dream, Bella," he whispered, and slowly pressed his lips to hers.

He felt her quick inhale and his own quick rush. Tasted the brightness of lemonade, the sweetness of strawberry.

He slid his fingers from her ponytail to the back of her neck and urged her closer.

Her fingers splayed against his chest. She murmured something against his lips. He barely heard. His head was full of sound. Full of pulse beats and bells.

She murmured again. This time not against his lips.

He frowned, feeling entirely thwarted. "What?"

She pulled back yet another inch. Her fingertips pushed instead of urged closer. "Do you want to answer that?"

It made sense then. His cell phone was ringing.

Don't miss
Cowboy in Disguise *by Allison Leigh,*
available June 2021 wherever
Harlequin Special Edition books and ebooks are sold.

Harlequin.com

HSEEXP0521